The Princess Sister Swap

Clem Beaumont and Princess Arrosa Artega, half sisters united by a strong and loving bond but kept apart by circumstances beyond their control. With pressure growing on Arrosa to marry, Clem hatches an audacious plan to temporarily swap their lives, giving Arrosa one final summer of freedom in Cornwall and allowing Clem to spend time in the beautiful country of Asturia, a place denied to her all of her life!

But their simple—if risky—plan begins to unravel when Arrosa and Clem unexpectedly meet the men of their dreams...

Read Clem and Akil's story in
Cinderella and the Vicomte
Available now

And don't miss Arrosa and Jack's story
Coming soon from Harlequin Romance

Dear Reader,

I love a life-swap story, the opportunity for a character to step into someone else's shoes and see if the grass really is greener. And what if the shoes belonged to a princess, to your very own half sister? That's the opportunity that awaits Clem in the first story in my The Princess Sister Swap duet. When she sees that her sister needs some time away from royal duties, she jumps at the chance to explore the life that might have been hers.

Up-and-coming politician Akil is facing a huge decision, one that will change the rest of his life, and the last thing he needs is an instant connection with state-secret, scandal-in-waiting Clem. But after their first encounter, he finds he can't stop thinking about her and soon has to decide which matters more—his career and the vow he made to his father or his growing feelings for Clem.

I loved writing about these two lonely people brought together by fate. I hope you love it, too.

Love,

Jessica

Cinderella and the Vicomte

———

Jessica Gilmore

ISBN-13: 978-1-335-40708-5

Cinderella and the Vicomte

Harlequin Enterprises ULC
22 Adelaide St. West, 41st Floor
Toronto, Ontario M5H 4E3, Canada
www.Harlequin.com

Printed in U.S.A.

Incorrigible lover of a happy-ever-after, **Jessica Gilmore** is lucky enough to work for one of London's best-known theaters. Married with one daughter, one fluffy dog and two dog-loathing cats, she can usually be found with her nose in a book. Jessica writes emotional romance with a hint of humor, a splash of sunshine, delicious food—and equally delicious heroes!

Books by Jessica Gilmore

Harlequin Romance

Billion-Dollar Matches

Indonesian Date with the Single Dad

Fairytale Brides

Cinderella's Secret Royal Fling
Reawakened by His Christmas Kiss
Bound by the Prince's Baby

Wedding Island

Baby Surprise for the Spanish Billionaire

Summer Romance with the Italian Tycoon
Mediterranean Fling to Wedding Ring
Winning Back His Runaway Bride
Christmas with His Cinderella

Visit the Author Profile page
at Harlequin.com for more titles.

For Jess

See you in SF x

**Praise for
Jessica Gilmore**

"Totally loved every page. I was hooked right into the story, reading every single word. This book has to be my new favourite. Honestly this book is most entertaining."

—*Goodreads* on *Honeymooning with Her Brazilian Boss*

CHAPTER ONE

"'For never was a story of more woe, than this of Juliet and her Romeo.'"

For one breathless moment the silence seemed overwhelming and then, like one of the waves crashing onto the shore behind her, loud applause rang out. Clemence Beaumont lay perfectly still for one last second as the still-real emotion swirled through her and then, as reality started to return, she raised her head and allowed Ed, her co-star, to pull her to her feet, letting the dagger fall to the floor. Taking his hand, she walked to the front of the curved stage, the rest of the cast falling in behind them, and bowed. Straightening with a grin, she took in the audience for the first time since she'd stepped onto the stage in answer to the nurse's call.

Semicircular seating rose up away from the stage, the outdoor theatre more amphitheatre than traditional auditorium, respectably full for an amateur fundraising performance. Clem bowed again as the whoops and cheers rang out, the welcome and much-missed post-performance adrenaline flooding her veins. Blinking, she started to make out individuals in the crowd: her best friend, Sally, who must have found a babysitter after all; Mrs Atkins, her favourite primary school teacher, beaming away; Mr Reynolds, her English teacher, nodding at her in approval, he adored Shakespeare and tried to make sure all his pupils did too; her neighbour Trinny, dressed to the nines as always; her sister…

Hang on. Her gaze skittered back. Her *sister*? Arrosa was *here*, in Cornwall? How had she managed to get away—not just get away but also seemingly alone? Clem couldn't see her bodyguard anywhere although she knew Henri couldn't be far behind. Arrosa hadn't gone out in public without the special-service-trained protection officer in the last decade.

Her seatmates didn't seem to have recognised her although her face regularly adorned front pages and gossip sites, probably thanks to the hat pulled low over her sleek, dark curls and the thick-rimmed glasses shading her face, but Clem would have recognised her in twice the disguise. After all, a similar face looked out at her from the mirror every morning. The sisters shared the same cheekbones and nose, the same dimples and long-lashed hazel eyes. But whereas Arrosa was a princess, legitimate daughter of King Zorien of Asturia, Clem was the unplanned result of a gap-year romance, her existence hidden away from half her family and the country her father ruled. A country she had never even visited.

She continued to bow and smile mechanically, but her mind was no longer on the performance and applause. What on *earth* was her sister doing here? Clem had sent her an invite of course, but she hadn't actually expected her to come. She never had before. It was hard for Arrosa to get away.

Finally, the applause came to an end and the cast filed backstage, chattering loudly as the post-production euphoria spread through all the crew and actors.

'Everyone back to ours,' Ed proclaimed, his arm around Tybalt, normally known as Tom and Ed's other half. 'Clem? Ready to party?'

'It's not that I don't want to...' she started, and his face softened.

'You were sensational tonight, Clem, and you should celebrate. I know it's not the same, but she'd want you to.'

Not the same without her mother, he meant. Simone Beaumont had produced and directed many of the village plays, been at the forefront of the restoration campaign that had transformed the neglected open-air theatre. If she were still alive she would be spearheading the Save Our Theatre battle against a local developer who wanted to change the beloved community asset into yet another commercial venture catering to tourists. Her mother had loved a cause. Clem had lost count of all her campaigns and passions long ago. It had used to infuriate her, feeling that her own feelings and needs came second to whatever—or whoever—her mother was championing at the time, but now she would give anything to walk into the kitchen and see her mother furiously making a placard— *Save the Seals*, *Save the Birds*, *Clean up the Sewage*, *Save our Post Office*. Simone Beaumont. Champion of the underdog.

'We'll give you a lift,' Tom added, but Clem shook her head.

'I'll try and make it, but I think I saw my cousin in the audience.'

'Bring them along.'

'I'll see what she says. We don't see each other often so she may want to catch up at home. Enjoy the party. You were both brilliant tonight, thank you.' She kissed both men on the cheek and headed off to change. She'd been looking forward to the post-show celebration but knew her promise to try and make it wouldn't be fulfilled. It had been a long time since Arrosa had dared to be seen publicly with her, or even attend a party without prior clearance; her half-sister might have the title, a luxurious lifestyle, more money than Clem could imagine, and a real relationship with their father, but Clem knew she had a freedom Arrosa could never have.

She changed quickly and removed her stage make-up and within fifteen minutes she made her way out of the theatre to walk the short distance home. She'd been born and brought up in the pretty coastal village her mother had moved to after she'd found out that her lover wasn't just a fellow student at the Sorbonne, but a prince with an arranged marriage due to take place imminently. Three months after moving to Cornwall Simone gave birth alone in a strange town—and six months later the birth of a new princess was celebrated in Asturia. Clem couldn't imagine how alone her mother must have felt, an orphan, single mother and betrayed lover. But she knew that Simone had loved the curve of the harbour, the pretty fishermen's cottages that clustered up the cliff, the wide sweep of beach, and Clem did too; she wouldn't swap her home for any palace. Which was a good thing because here she was, recalled home by her mother's long, lingering illness.

In the six months since her mother had died Clem had toyed with the idea of returning to London, to keep trying to make it as a professional actress, but making any decision seemed too hard, her grief still paralyzingly raw. In a world where she had no one, leaving the familiarity of home was more than she could manage.

She turned in at the small path that led to the cottage Zorien had bought them all those years ago. Clem hadn't been able to bring herself to change a thing. Her mother's clothes still hung in her wardrobe; her wax jacket swung from her peg in the hallway.

Arrosa had her own key and when Clem

walked into the sitting room, her sister was curled up on the sofa. She'd discarded the hat and glasses, her long dark curls tumbling free, her expression thoughtful and more than a little wistful as she stared into the unlit fireplace. She looked up as Clem opened the door, jumping to her feet and rushing over to give Clem a warm hug.

'It's not that I'm not happy to see you, Rosy, but what on earth are you doing here?' Clem asked as she accepted a glass of the excellent wine Arrosa had brought with her and inspected the delicious array of goodies spread out on the coffee table, more crammed inside the Fortnum & Mason's hamper by her feet. She selected a piece of cheese and sat back.

'Apart from watching my sister play Juliet? Clem, you were brilliant.' Arrosa's English was perfect thanks to a British nanny and five years in an English boarding school, with no trace of an accent unless she was emotional or excited. Which was a shame. Clem loved her sister's accent, a reminder of the country she had never known. The small and much contested independent kingdom was positioned between France and Spain and the dialect was close to French, but the accent owed more to their Spanish neighbour.

'You've never come to see me act before.'

Arrosa curled back up on the sofa. 'I wish I had. Clem, I'm so sorry I didn't come to Simone's funeral. I loved her so much, but…'

'That's okay, she would have understood. And you sent such beautiful flowers.'

'But you're my sister, I should have been there for you.'

'It's hard for you to get away. I know that.' But Clem had looked for her that long, sad day and her absence had hurt. Clem wasn't lying, she *did* understand the restrictions on their relationship, but there were times she was tired of being the skeleton in the family cupboard. Of shouldering life's burdens alone.

'It was easier when we were children. Especially when I was at school and could spend my exeat weekends here as well as some of the holidays.'

Some people might have found it strange that Simone had agreed to Zorien's request that Arrosa spend time with them anonymously, posing as Clem's cousin so that she could get to know her sister, but Simone, with her trick of embracing lost causes, had taken one look at Arrosa and enfolded her into the family. 'A palace is no place to raise a child,' she would say. 'She needs some fun, to be allowed to run wild.' And run wild they had, long halcyon beach days drenched in sun and sea.

Halcyon days that had ended as they'd left their teens and Arrosa had had to take on state duties. Now they barely got the chance to meet, their long weekly phone calls their sole communication.

And Arrosa hadn't mentioned anything about a visit the last time they spoke just a few days ago.

'Fess up, why are you here apart from coming to see me as Juliet? Don't think I'm not pleased to see you, but I know you and impulsive isn't in your schedule. Is everything okay?'

Arrosa took a swig of wine, a shadow passing over her face. 'I'm not sure. I think I just asked someone to marry me.'

'You think or you did? Are congratulations in order?' Clem tried to keep the surprise off her face. She was sure there was no one special in Arrosa's life. No one *not* special either. Asturia was a small patriarchal society with old-fashioned values and their Crown Princess was supposed to embody those values. 'Who is the lucky man?'

'Akil. He's the Vicomte d'Ortiz, a rising star of the opposition. His father, the Duc d'Ortiz, was one of Papa's most vocal critics. Our families have been enemies for generations, you know how Asturians can be, but Akil and I are friends of a sort. We have a lot in common. Family honour and expectations and that kind of thing.'

'Friends? You're not even dating? Is this a friends-to-lovers thing? Rosy, marriage is a big first step. Why not start off with dinner and a film? Besides…' Clem topped up their wine glasses before turning to face her sister '…what do you mean you *think* you asked him to marry you?'

Arrosa reddened. 'Akil has been instrumental into getting the opposition parties to agree to the change in law that will allow me to inherit the throne. You know, it's really important that there's consensus, it's such a change. Asturia is so traditional that any hint of controversy, even a politician voting against the change, could make it harder for the people to accept me.'

Arrosa had told Clem more than once how relieved she was that the Asturian primogeniture laws meant she would never have to become Queen, but when it had become clear that no son would succeed him, her father—their father—had thrown himself into changing the law. Now, eight years later they were just weeks away from the law being ratified and Arrosa becoming the official heir to the throne. Whatever Arrosa's personal feelings about her new destiny, she had shouldered the change with her usual, intelligent grace.

'Oh, now I get it, in return for his help he gets half the kingdom and the Princess's hand in marriage. That still is the going rate?'

But Arrosa didn't answer her teasing smile, taking another sip of her wine as she stared pensively into the empty fireplace. 'Clem, everyone—my parents, my advisers, the newspapers—has been pushing me to marry. To start thinking about an heir of my own. And the country will see me as more settled, more mature, if I am married. I don't like being rushed, but I see the sense in it. The problem is, not only am I single, but I don't see that changing. On the rare occasion I meet someone I like the whole princess thing scares them off. Queen-to-be is going to make that a hundred times worse. I like Akil, and he understands the court and my world, and we have similar ambitions for Asturia… We were talking about what I wanted to achieve as the heir and realised how aligned our goals were, and I suddenly thought, well, he's the right age, single, understands my world. I could do a lot worse.'

'So you asked him if he'd do you the honour?' She knew the situation wasn't funny, but humour was all that Clem had right now. Pity wouldn't help anyone, least of all her sister.

'Not exactly. I just said maybe he'd achieve more as Prince Consort and then fled the scene in mortification. What if he says yes?'

'Do you *want* him to say yes?'

'It's not what I dreamed of as a little girl. But it *would* make things easier.'

'The last of the true romantics. What's he like? Is he good-looking?' Other words hovered unsaid—is he kind, will he respect you, can you fall in love with him?

'I think so. He's pleasant enough to look at.'

Arrosa handed over her phone to Clem, who sucked in a breath. *Pleasant enough to look at?* Understatement of the century. With cheekbones sharp enough to slice through ice, a determined chin, sensuous mouth and a knowing glint in dark eyes, the Vicomte was film-star handsome. And if Arrosa couldn't see that then she really shouldn't marry him.

'Yes, pleasant enough,' she said wryly.

'He's a good man.' Was Arrosa trying to convince Clem—or herself?

'But?'

Arrosa rubbed her eyes. 'Queens make sacrifices for the common good. I know that. But I'm giving up any last hope of privacy, of choosing my own path. Is marrying someone I don't love one sacrifice too many? Being the monarch is lonely enough. It would be easier with a real partner by my side. Someone who wants to marry me because of me, not my title. But I'm not sure that person is out there. Akil is a sensible choice. Maybe that should be enough.'

'Rosy, I think this is something you need to take some time and think about. Really think about.' In fact, she shouldn't be making any decisions while she was clearly overwhelmed. Clem had never seen her sister so pale, never seen such huge shadows under her eyes or her usually laughter-filled face so solemn. 'You need a break.'

Arrosa sighed. 'I know. It's been intense. But don't worry, I'm slowing down for the summer, I've cleared my diary for the next few weeks leading up to the ratification as things will get really busy once I'm confirmed. Papa wants me to take on some decision-making duties straight away. There's a lot to learn. He's still young, but of course he inherited the throne long before he thought he would. He wants me to be ready.'

'A break? So you'll go on holiday?'

Her smile was wan. 'I wouldn't go that far. There's a lot to do, to organise, but at least I've got no engagements or formal meetings.'

'Then organise it from here.' Clem turned to her sister eagerly. 'Stay here for a few weeks, Rosy. You know the Cornish air does you good.' And then they could spend some real time together. Maybe for the last time.

'I'd love to,' Arrosa said wistfully. 'But I'm heading back tonight.'

'Tonight? Oh, Rosy.' Disappointment hit Clem hard. She hadn't realised how lonely she was until she had seen her sister sitting high up in the amphitheatre. She had friends, lots of them, but nobody who was hers alone.

How she wished she and Arrosa could actually *be* sisters properly. Have more than a weekly phone call and a few snatched hours here and there.

'I know, but I'll be missed if I'm gone too long.'

'You said yourself that you have no meetings.'

'I don't, but the speculation if I'm not seen even from the distance could be damaging this close to the ratification. I didn't go anywhere for a couple of weeks when I had flu last year and according to the tabloids I was having a facelift, had joined a cult and eloped with a soldier. I know it's silly and I shouldn't care but it's not just that I don't want any rumours circulating at home—eventually the press would find me and then they'd start wondering who *you* are and that's the last thing you need. It's safest for you if we're not seen together, Clem.'

'*If* they find you. After all, why would they look for you here?' But Clem knew all too well that Arrosa was always tracked down eventually. Once Arrosa had turned eighteen the press had turned their lenses on her and she had become a front-page staple. There weren't many beautiful, young single princesses around and what she wore and ate, who she spoke to and where she went were all put under intense scrutiny.

But no one in Cornwall had ever realised that the child and teenager who spent so many holidays with the Beaumonts was the Asturian Princess. In fact, some of Clem's friends and neighbours still asked after her cousin. People saw what they expected to see, and nobody expected to see a European princess eating ice cream on a Cornish beach. And look at her! Worryingly pale and thin. She obviously needed a proper holiday. One here in the Cornish air. Time away from politics and diplomacy and Court. Time to decide if marrying someone because he had done her a good turn and understood her world was really what she wanted.

Maybe there was a way to make it happen.

'I could go back to Asturia in your place,' Clem said slowly, trying the words on for size.

Arrosa started to laugh but the sound died away as her eyes grew big with shock. 'You're serious? Clem, no one would ever think you were me.'

'Up close, no, but in the back of a car, hair all neat like you, in your clothes, with those big sunglasses you wear… Why wouldn't they? People see what they expect to see.' She repeated the words she'd just thought, the truth of them becoming clearer with every second. 'We're the same build and height, the same colouring. And I'm an actress, I can walk like you, hold myself like you. You could have the summer here and I'll spend it in Asturia making sure the press get enough glimpses to think you're busy preparing for the ratification, leaving you free to get some serious relaxation. I talk about my cousin all the time. No one here will think anything of it if we say I've got a job and you're cat-sitting. The only unbelievable part will be that I've been cast in anything. I'll have to claim I ended up on the cutting-room floor.'

'That's the craziest thing I've ever heard. We'd never get away with it.'

A tendril of hope in Arrosa's voice made Clem push away her own doubts.

'If you lived in the main castle or had dozens of servants then I agree, it would be impossible…'

'But I have my own cottage in the grounds of the Palais d'Artega,' Arrosa said slowly. 'I make my own meals when I'm there, people do come in to clean but not when I'm around. Only Marie is there regularly, but of course she and Henri would need to know if there was any chance of this succeeding… But it would be lonely, Clem. You'd have to be careful that no maids, no gardeners, no staff at all saw you. Some are new but some have been at the palais since I was a baby. What would you do with yourself?'

Lonely. That was a state Clem had got all too used to over the last year and a half. 'I'll make sure the press see Henri drive me around, dressed as you, of course, but in between I'll wear my own clothes, let my hair go back to natural wildness and explore Asturia incognito. I've always wanted to go but somehow I never have.' She'd always hoped that Zorien would find a way to invite her over, but of course he had always said it was too risky. 'It would be a chance for me to see our father too. It'd be easier for him to spend time with me if I'm living at yours. No one would question him visiting you.' She tried to keep the bitterness from her voice. She knew Zorien was a distant father to Arrosa in many ways too, but at least they had a real relationship, not just an awkward meeting every few years. She was grateful for the cottage and for the money he'd settled on her but would gladly swap both for a real father.

'But what's the point of me being here if you aren't?'

'Well, Gus needs feeding, for a start.' Clem pointed at the slim black cat occupying the window seat. 'The sea needs swimming in, scones need eating, beaches need walking on and you need time to be you, not the Crown Princess and future Queen. This gives you that time. And I need a change of scene too. I've been putting off making plans for my future, just existing for too long. Maybe some time away will give me some much-needed perspective. You'd be doing me a favour.'

'Sure, *I'd* be doing *you* the favour.' Arrosa shook her head affectionately at Clem.

'We'll do each other a favour. We both need some time away from our lives, so why not swap for a while? Your mother's not at home, is she?' She knew that Iara Artega rarely spent much time in the Artega country estate, preferring to spend her time socialising in the small capital or journeying abroad.

'No, she's spending the summer on Ischia on a retreat.'

'Then we're safe.' Arrosa's mother knew

about Clem, but the two had never met and Clem sensed the Queen would prefer to keep it that way. 'We could do this. Your call, Rosy. What will it be? Six weeks of avoiding Akil, ducking away from the press and worrying yourself into a shadow or all the cream teas you can eat and a summer lazing on the beach?'

'We must be mad to even consider this would work.' But there was a hint of the old fire in Arrosa's eyes and Clem knew she was close to agreeing.

'It's easy enough to swap back if we need to,' she pointed out and Arrosa nodded then laughed.

'You're right. Let's give it a week and see where we are. Thank you, Clem. Cornwall is just what I need, and I think maybe Asturia is where you need to be as well. To a change of scenery.' She held up her glass and Clem clinked it with hers.

'To the princess swap.'

CHAPTER TWO

AKIL STRODE ACROSS the ornate hallway and into the formal receiving room. His own taste ran to simple but the decor in his ancestral home had clearly not got the memo. Gilt and marble prevailed, every piece of furniture was priceless, old and incredibly uncomfortable and portraits of bewigged disapproving ancestors glared down from every wall.

Every one of them no doubt had an opinion on the dilemma he'd not been able to stop turning over and over since his last conversation with Arrosa had taken an unexpected turn.

It was an enticing prospect, an effortless climb to the very top of Asturia but, then again, he was doing pretty fine as he was. More than fine: Shadow Minister of the Interior at thirty with the possibility of making it to party leader before forty, a decade before his father had achieved the title. And as leader of the opposition, maybe even First Minister one day if the swing away from the traditionalists continued, Akil would wield a lot of power, the kind of power he had been born and bred to wield. But in Asturia the throne still held a lot of influence and nothing happened without the court's approval.

And that was the heart of his dilemma. Because he couldn't deny that if he were right next to the throne, married to a woman he knew shared many of his ideals, then together they could enact real change. The change so desperately needed if Asturia was ever to move forward, to be more than a curious little country sandwiched between France and Spain, a pub quiz answer and a quirky holiday destination. More, it would ensure that Ortiz blood would run in the veins of future kings and queens. He knew what his father would say. He would tell him to stop hesitating and act. Propose formally and marry her before she had a chance to change her mind.

But it wasn't that simple. He liked Arrosa, admired her grace and intelligence, appreciated her beauty, but he didn't *know* her, not in the way he should know a woman he was considering marrying. Akil knew that he needed to marry carefully, strategically; after all, as his mother knew to her cost, being married to a politician meant sacrifices. But he did want compatibility. Companionship. Not the chilly battleground he'd grown up in.

Blinking, his eyes readjusted as the door swung shut behind him. The heavy velvet drapes were pulled against the midday sun, the large, dark room dimly lit by lamps. His mother lay on a chaise, barely mustering a smile as Akil walked over and bowed over her outstretched hand.

'You look more like your father every day.' It wasn't a compliment.

'Mama.' He suppressed a grimace and sat down on the low stool beside her. 'You look well.'

'That's very kind of you, *cheri*.' Her tone made it clear that she didn't find him kind at all. His mother made a study of ill health and excelled, but Akil found it hard to indulge her when, thanks to his volunteering work, he saw real ill people in the overstretched public hospitals. 'But my head has been bad recently. I thought you knew, but of course you are so busy, how could you remember such an insignificant detail?' Her sigh was perfectly calculated to sit midway between heartbroken and plaintive.

It should be perfectly calculated. She'd worked on it long enough.

Nerea Ortiz was still nearer fifty than sixty, her dark hair owing more to nature than her hairdresser's art, her figure still slim and toned, her face unlined. But she reclined as if she were a Victorian great-aunt, a small, fat lapdog snoring at her feet, a shawl around her shoulders and a selection of herbal remedies cluttering up a small table that also held a china cup half filled with weak tea and a matching plate holding two wafer-thin biscuits. A water bottle sat on another table—that was if it was water. Early as it was, it could easily be gin.

Not for the first time, Akil thought that his mother lived in entirely the wrong era.

'I'm sorry to hear that,' he said with the patience born of long practice. 'But I'm here now and I can assure you that you have my full attention.'

Akil managed a dutiful hour by his mother's side before pleading work duties and taking his leave. As he left the room his eye was caught by a photo. His mother at twenty, beautiful and glowing, full of life. It was easy to forget that when Akil had been young, very young, she had been that vibrant young woman. But years of his father's disapproval and dislike had worn away all her *joie de vivre* until ill health became her only defence against her husband's scathing tongue. His weapons were anger and contempt, sarcasm and noise, hers tears and shrinking, martyrdom and illness.

And drink. Never spoken about, never acknowledged, all too often present.

No wonder Akil had spent as much of his childhood and now adulthood elsewhere, only coming back to the Ortiz ancestral home when duty commanded. Now he was the head of the family he had to visit more often but had resisted moving back to the place where he had been so unhappy, his father's disappointment still reverberating in every room. Although, since recovering from the heart attack that had felled him eight years ago, his father now spent most of his time in the family's Swiss villa.

Apparently not alone.

Akil sighed. Thoughts of his father were always complicated: guilt, dislike and yet, still, that frustrating, inexplicable and yet ever-present need to make him proud— and to beat him. To show that Akil had everything it took to be the Duc, the head of the family, to bear the Ortiz name. His father had always urged Akil to marry tactically. 'Don't let your head get turned by some pretty lightweight like I did,' he'd told Akil more than once. 'Marry a woman who brings influence and power. Who can further the family cause.' Who better than the Crown Princess?

The beep of his phone recalled him to his surroundings and Akil paused on the top of the wide stone steps that led from the grand double-height entrance way down to the curved driveway. He pulled his phone out of his pocket and glared at the screen, the tension leaving his body when he saw the name on it.

Elixane.

'Hey, what's up?' He walked slowly down the steps, an invisible load lifting more with every inch he moved away from the house. His car was right in front of him but he carried on, turning onto a gravelled path that ran across the front of the house and into the walled garden, which had been Akil's favourite hiding place as a small boy.

'I meant to return your call before now but things have been crazy,' his sister said. 'Everything okay?'

Akil hesitated. He'd called Elixane right after Arrosa had—possibly, maybe—suggested he consider becoming her Prince Consort, desperate to talk the conversation over with someone, but the more time passed, the less he felt able to articulate what had been said. 'Everything's fine.' He paused. 'I've just visited Mama.'

'How is she?'

'Much the same.'

She sighed. 'That's not good. I did try and suggest she drank less last time I saw her, but she pretended she didn't know what I was talking about. It isn't even the quantity I worry about, it's the drinking alone. How about Papa?'

'Last I heard he was much the same too.'

'You mean he's also drinking too much and eating too much and probably spending too much time with the mistresses we're not supposed to know the old hypocrite has, while you fulfil his dreams for him?'

She had a point. 'He nearly died.'

'Of bad temper. Eight years ago.'

'Early retirement was the best option.'

'For who? Not for you, that's for sure. I still can't believe he guilted you into dropping your studies to take over from him.'

'Elixane,' Akil said warningly. 'I made my own decisions then and I make my own decisions now.'

'Which is why I'm the one doing a surgical residency in New York?'

'And I couldn't be happier for you.' He stepped through the small, hidden archway that led into the garden and the last of the tension left him as he entered. Old, twisted fruit trees covered with fresh green leaves, blossom petals carpeting the grass, little winding paths darting between them, wildflowers populating the grass.

'Now what can I say to that?' Elixane complained. 'Maybe you are better off as a politician. You always know what to say.'

'Not always. I had an interesting conversation with the Princess the other day and I had no idea how to respond,' he said, his eyes fixed on a bee busily divesting a flower of nectar. 'She's being pressured to marry.'

'Poor Arrosa, I can just imagine.' Elixane was the same age as the Princess and despite the family rivalry the girls had been friends of a sort growing up. 'You're in the Senate, you know what that bunch of dinosaurs are like. They still think a woman needs a man's steadying hand. I don't envy her. She's got an uphill battle with that lot.'

'She recognises that. She's not afraid, but I think she feels it would be easier if she wasn't facing them alone. She...' He coughed, the words feeling as ridiculous as he knew they would sound. 'She asked how I felt about being the Prince Consort.'

'She *what*? She *proposed*?' Elixane's voice rose to shrill frequency and Akil winced. 'To *you*? I didn't know you two were that close.'

'We're not, and no.' Akil wasn't sure exactly what had happened in that conversation, but he was sure about that. 'She didn't propose exactly. It was more of a sounding me out, I think.'

'And you said how flattering but no thank you.'

'I didn't say anything.' He hadn't had a chance to formulate any kind of response before Arrosa had blushed furiously, made an excuse and left.

'My brother a prince. That would bring Papa hotfooting it home from Switzerland. But it's ridiculous, of course. Please let me be there when you tell him you had the chance to marry into the royal family and turned it down.'

Akil didn't answer and Elixane's voice tightened. 'You are turning it down, aren't you?'

'I don't know. Not yet. I'd be a fool not to at least consider it, Elixane.'

'But, Akil, you don't love her. You barely know her!'

'I've spent some time with her recently and I like her. Respect her. Besides, love isn't necessary for a happy marriage.'

'Love doesn't guarantee a happy marriage but it sure as hell helps. You can't base your decisions on the disaster that's our parents' marriage. They didn't love each other. They were infatuated and that's a whole different ball game.'

'Love or infatuation, it's undeniable that everything they wanted and needed in a marriage was incompatible and I will never make that mistake.' Never raise children amongst the hostility and unhappiness of a toxic marriage. 'If I marry, then I need a politician's wife, someone diplomatic, intelligent, with shared goals. Why not Arrosa? Being part of the court rather than parliament would be a different kind of politics but together we could achieve great things.'

'At what cost?'

'There's always a cost to power, Elixane. You just need to decide what you're willing to pay.'

'I haven't seen Arrosa for years,' his sister said after a long pause. 'We were friendly but not close. She's not close to anyone as far as I know, but I liked her. Like her. She's nice.'

'Yes,' Akil agreed. 'She's nice.'

'And that's enough?'

Akil leaned against a tree. 'It's a hell of a lot better than not nice,' he pointed out. 'Look, we both want this country to move beyond ancient feuds, we want a modern democracy.'

'And marriage is the only way to achieve that?' Akil could hear the scepticism in his sister's voice. 'It's the twenty-first century.'

Akil couldn't help his wry smile. 'In the rest of Europe maybe, but you know as well as I do that for over half this country it might as well be the seventeenth century.'

'You know what I think you should do?'

'Do I want to know what you think?'

'I think you're insane and you shouldn't

give this any more thought, but if this is something you are really considering then you should get to really know her. Don't make any decisions either way until you've spent some time with the woman, not the Princess. Make sure this marriage is something that you both can live with.'

Another fat bee buzzed past Akil's ear before landing on a climbing rose. Akil watched it move from flower to flower as he considered his sister's words. He didn't know what he felt about Arrosa's surprising proposition or if she had even meant it. Spending some time with her when they weren't working on bills and treatises might be the way to find out if they were compatible. 'You may be right.'

'I *know* I'm right. You might think that you don't have to fall in love with her, but you have to admit that you need to know that you can live with her.'

Elixane's words hung in the air until a beep reminded Akil that he had a meeting to get to. 'Look, I've got to go. Thank you.'

'Call me if you need me. Any time.'

And with that she was gone. Akil pocketed his phone, frowning. His little sister was annoyingly right. If Arrosa had meant those softly spoken words—and if he was truly considering agreeing—then they needed to see if they could live in harmony. His parents' marriage was an example of everything he didn't want: thwarted passion, disappointment, anger and resentment. He wanted civilised, compatible and mutual respect. Maybe it was time to stop thinking and talk to Arrosa, discover if she had been serious and then decide what, if anything, that meant for him.

Before Akil left the Palais d'Ortiz he cancelled his morning meetings, and instead of heading back to the city drove further out into the countryside towards the huge Artega estate. He'd hesitated over whether he should ask his assistant to forewarn Arrosa that he was on his way; after all, even a rising politician working closely with the Princess shouldn't just rock up uninvited at a royal residence. But if he and Arrosa were to discuss something as important as marriage then surely they should be able to discuss it without formality and pomp—and a possible fiancé shouldn't need to make an appointment to see his intended.

Akil had visited Arrosa at home enough times to be waved through by the guards at the gate and he drove up the long, tree-lined drive, past the imposing chateau with its fairy-tale turrets and intricate stonework and headed towards the villa half a kilometre away where Arrosa resided. As he pulled up in front of the pretty white one-storey building he felt a momentary pang of unaccustomed doubt. Whatever they discussed here would set the tone for the rest of his life and he still didn't know what the outcome would be—or what he wanted it to be.

The nineteenth-century villa had an idyllic setting with its lakeside location and flower-filled gardens, a small orchard to one side. But despite the peaceful pastoral feeling, Akil knew that at least one secret service agent would be concealed somewhere close by, and that CCTV cameras meant that his every move would be fed back to the soldiers at the gate. It was a sobering thought; he was used to living with a certain degree of high security, thanks to his father's position and now his own, and he had spent time himself in the special forces during his national service, but he had never been watched twenty-four-seven.

Unexpected pity for the Princess flooded through him; never alone, never private and now asking a man she surely didn't love to be her husband.

Akil strode down the paved garden path to the front door and knocked on it. The last couple of times he been here either Arrosa herself had opened it or her maid, Marie, would usher him in. Arrosa had no live-in staff at the villa. In fact she lived a surprisingly self-sufficient life; apart from the staff who ran her office from the court in the capital city her only permanent staff were Marie and her bodyguard.

He waited but nobody answered the door, although he could see several open windows and hear the sound of music from within the house. He rapped on the door once again and when there was still no answer headed around to the back of the villa. The long, terraced garden led down to the lake, where he could see a small boathouse and changing hut positioned by a short wooden jetty. Arrosa sat on the jetty, her back to him, her hair cascading down, wilder than he'd ever seen it before.

She didn't turn as he made his way down the garden towards her and Akil hesitated before he called out, not wanting to startle her.

'Arrosa,' he said softly and saw her whole

body stiffen. 'I did knock but nobody answered. I'm sorry to show up without notice.' Every sense told him that something wasn't quite right; he felt wrong-footed with no idea why. 'But what I have to say is too important to wait, and under the circumstances I felt some informality was warranted. I hope it goes without saying that I very much enjoy working with you, and I hope whatever happens that we will continue to work together over the years ahead. I have also come to value your companionship, friendship almost.'

Arrosa didn't speak, nor did she turn to face him. He couldn't read her body language at all. She was still rigid, like a deer scenting a predator, unsure whether to run or try to fade into the background.

'But marriage is a big commitment and not something either of us should enter into lightly,' he continued. 'If you didn't mean what you said the other day, if I misread your intention, or if you changed your mind, then I'll leave right now with no hard feelings and a promise never to mention it again. But if you did mean it then I think we need to spend some time together without titles between us, without work as a commonality, to see how compatible we are when all that is stripped away.'

Something about her stillness made it hard for him to let the silence fall but he made himself stop, wait for her to respond as the silence lengthened, the tension thickening with every long second until finally she spoke.

'Thank you.'

Akil frowned, that sense of wrongness intensifying. Just two words but they sounded off, her voice lower, her accent subtly different.

'But now isn't a good time…' she continued slowly. 'Could we do this later?' She hesitated. It was as if she was measuring every word. 'I know this is important.'

Was she ill? Upset? Hurt? Akil couldn't just walk away without knowing Arrosa was all right. Princess or no princess, possible fiancée or not, she was a human being without many people to confide in. Whatever the future held, he could at least be her friend. Akil stepped onto the narrow wooden jetty and in a few decisive strides reached the still seated figure.

'Arrosa? What's wrong?' He squatted next to her and touched her shoulder, turning her gently towards him. But her face was at once familiar and yet strange. There was the same dark waving hair, the same hazel eyes, although these were subtly lighter, more gold than brown, the same olive skin, even that same tilt to the nose adding personality to a face that otherwise could have been blandly beautiful, and the same full mouth.

But this was not the Princess. This was not Arrosa.

His hand dropped and he straightened, taking an instinctive step back. 'Where's the Princess—and who on earth are you?'

CHAPTER THREE

CLEM STAYED COMPLETELY still for another long moment, unsure how to play this. She had no script, no director's notes. It was a good thing she had done so many improvisations but unfortunately this time she had no idea what her part should be.

After all, less than twenty-four hours ago she had been readying herself to play Juliet with no plans beyond the play and the party. But in the end she'd barely had time to remind Arrosa to water the plants and feed the cat, before finding herself hustled into the car that had brought Arrosa to Cornwall and whisked off to the private jet her sister had commandeered. It had been long past midnight when she'd arrived at the Palais d'Artega and Henri had shown her to the pretty lakeside villa Arrosa had moved into on her twenty-first birthday where, despite all her excitement and trepidation, she had fallen asleep straight away. No opportunity to have second thoughts or wonder how this madcap scheme might work in practice.

No opportunity until now. Unfortunately she had still been trying to get her thoughts in order when Akil Ortiz had inconsiderately shown up and complicated an already difficult situation. Who just showed up without calling first? Especially when calling on a princess?

However, she did know one thing. She wasn't having this conversation sitting down. Slowly she clambered to her feet and brushed the dust off her skirt before tilting her chin and turning to face Akil, meeting his suspicious gaze squarely, only to falter as she took him in.

If her first thought was, *Wow, that photo really didn't do him justice*, then her second was *Lucky, lucky Arrosa*.

Clem had been to one of the UK's most prestigious drama schools and as a result some of her classmates were now global heart-throbs. But not one of the attractive charismatic men she'd studied with, acted with, and sometimes dated had anything near the sheer magnetism of the Asturian Vicomte.

He was tall and broad, with his almost black hair ruthlessly swept back, but Clem could see hints of a rebellious wave in the strands that fell over his brow, strong brows framing keen dark brown eyes, a straight Roman nose turning his good looks characterful. His powerful body was showcased by a navy suit that had clearly been made to fit him, his olive skin set off by the crisp white of his linen open-collared shirt.

To her horror Clem felt a jolt of attraction pulsing low in her stomach, tingling through her whole body.

No, down, bad girl, she told herself fiercely as she summoned up her most regal smile, the one she'd used when playing Olivia in *Twelfth Night* during their third-year showcase.

'You must be the Vicomte d'Ortiz. I'm sorry, but Arrosa isn't here right now.'

'I see.' Suspicion lurked in his dark eyes as he surveyed her. 'When will she be back?'

'Not for a while. I'm house-sitting for her.' Did princesses who lived on their family estate surrounded by servants need house-sitters? Judging by the way Akil's eyes narrowed, he didn't think so. 'I needed a place for a while,' she added hurriedly. 'Really she's the one doing me the favour.'

'And you are?'

'Clem, Clemence Beaumont.' Surely knowing her name wouldn't do any harm? She wasn't linked anywhere with her father and sister. If he searched for her online all Akil would find would be some reviews of plays, her profile on her agent's website and her mother's obituary where Clem was buried beneath all the causes Simone had supported. 'I can let Arrosa know you dropped by, or you could tell her yourself, of course.'

'She didn't tell me she was going away.'

'It was all very sudden. And she doesn't want it to be common knowledge so please don't tell anyone.' She took a step forward but he didn't move. The only way past meant either brushing past him or going into the water and neither appealed. 'I'm sorry you had a wasted journey, but it was really nice to meet you,' she said pointedly. 'I'd offer you a coffee, but I really have to get on.'

If only that were true. Now she was here, Clem had no idea what to do next. Arrosa had promised to contact their father straight away to let him know what they were doing and she was anxiously hoping to hear from him. In the meantime her plans to explore had been thwarted by the realisation that Arrosa didn't have her own car and that she was driven everywhere by Henri. That was fine for the times she planned to dress as the Princess and be driven somewhere in order to make it seem as if Arrosa were here in Asturia, but the bulletproof limousine was far too conspicuous for her to use to be a tourist. Lovely as the villa was and inviting as the lake was, she didn't want to spend six weeks alone with nothing to do. She could do that back in Cornwall.

'You didn't say how you know Arrosa.' He clearly wasn't shifting. Maybe it was a good sign, this protectiveness. Although Arrosa already had a bodyguard watching her every move.

'No,' she said lightly. 'I didn't. Now if you'll excuse me.' He moved then, slowly and clearly reluctantly, and she slipped past him. 'I'm sure you can see your own way out. After all, you found your own way in.' She didn't look back as she headed up the path but she could feel his gaze boring into her as if he were trying to strip her secrets from her.

The garden was split onto three terraces. Lawn abutted the lake, then steps led up to a colourful flower-filled area, alive with bees and butterflies. The third terrace was paved with pots of plants providing shade and colour, an outdoor sofa and chairs on one side and a dining table and chairs on the other. It seemed to take an age to get to the French doors that led into the house and safety, and it wasn't until her hand was finally on the handle when he spoke.

'Wait.'

Reluctantly Clem turned. Akil had followed her onto the top terrace and he stood by the table, hands clenched.

'Just tell me, is Arrosa all right?'

Clem paused, trying to read him. Did he care about her sister as a person, or was he thinking about the power and influence she could give him?

But Arrosa had said that he was a good man and she was a shrewd judge of character. She'd had to be. And Clem had overheard words never meant for her ears after all. Words which, although she still wanted a lot more for her sister than a diplomatic convenient marriage, had gone a long way towards reassuring her that Akil wouldn't take advantage of her sister.

'She's fine.'

'Is there anything I can do to help? I got the impression the other day that she needed a friend. I hope she knows she can come to me if she's in trouble.'

It clearly cost him to ask the question, to look that vulnerable in front of a stranger, a stranger who he had already inadvertently spilled secrets to. The situation needed re-balancing. He deserved some truth from her. And this was a good chance for her to evaluate the man her sister definitely didn't love but thought of highly enough to consider entrusting her future happiness to.

'Maybe I do have time for a coffee after all,' she said. 'Do you?'

Clem still didn't know her way around her sister's well-appointed kitchen and it took some time to locate everything she needed and to load it onto a tray and carry it to the outside table where Akil awaited her. Despite her invitation, Akil hadn't sat; instead he stood at the edge of the terrace gazing out towards the lake. As Clem exited the house, he turned and quickly strode towards her, relieving her of the tray despite her protestations and setting it onto the wooden table. Clem followed him and took a seat, reaching for the cafetière gratefully. She was definitely in need of caffeine.

There was something peculiarly intimate about sitting opposite someone, asking them how they took their coffee, pouring it and adding the milk. Intimate and yet distancing, the lack of knowledge a sign that they were strangers. Although here at least she had the advantage. She knew who Akil was; he had no idea she even existed.

He accepted the coffee but made no move to drink it, instead setting the cup onto the table and looking at her with a frown. 'I spoke to Arrosa just two days ago and she made no mention of going away. The ratification is in just a couple of months' time. This is no time for her to disappear. What's going on?'

Clem sat back and regarded him steadily. 'Once the law has been ratified and Arrosa is officially the Crown Princess, how much time will she have to go away? How much privacy? She's already constrained in so many ways, guarded at all times, and it's only going to get worse. This is a perfect time for her to have some space. Maybe the last chance she has.'

He inclined his head briefly as if acknowledging her point. 'But that doesn't explain what you're doing here or who you are, Clemence Beaumont. I don't believe I've heard Arrosa mention you before.'

'Does Arrosa know all your friends?' Clem asked sweetly and only the slightest narrowing of his eyes showed his displeasure with her answer.

'Your resemblance to her is quite startling, too startling for it to be a coincidence although Beaumont is not an Asturian name. You must be related, but I know all her relatives around your age and you're not one of them.'

'You've done quite the study on her genealogy.'

To her surprise Akil laughed, transforming his face from an austere, remote handsomeness to something warmer—and dangerously attractive. 'Asturia is a small country and everybody knows everybody. And *I* know that I've never seen you before and I've not heard your name and so I'm wondering why someone who looks so like the Crown Princess is living in her house when the Crown Princess has unexpectedly disappeared.'

'You have a vivid imagination. You should write crime books.' Clem took a sip of coffee and smiled. 'But there's no mystery here. Text Arrosa, she will tell you that she is fine.'

'It just seems a strange coincidence that just a couple of days after our conversation she disappears.' He stopped then, his mouth tightening as if he'd realised that he'd said too much. But it was a little bit too late to pretend ignorance about the possible match between her sister and this disturbing man when she'd heard his opening speech.

'Look,' she said, setting her cup onto the table. 'I can't pretend I didn't hear what you said earlier, and I can't pretend that I don't know what you're talking about. I also can't comment on where Arrosa is or why she's there. That's her personal business and if you need to know more than that you should ask her. She has her phone. I spoke to her this morning. As for me, I'm here partly because, like Arrosa, I could do with some time away from my life, but mainly to give her this time. You know how hard it is for her to have any peace. As you said, we look alike, and from a distance, with the right hair and make-up, through the windows of her car most people would mistake me for her. If I make sure I'm seen dressed as her two or three times a week from a distance, then nobody will think to go looking for her. I'm giving her the space she needs. Nothing more sinister than that.'

Without taking his eyes off her Akil pulled out his phone and dictated a quick message.

Arrosa, I'm at your house with Clem, let me know everything's all right.

He put his phone down. 'Okay, that's why you're here. But I still don't know who you are, or that I can trust you.'

'Arrosa trusts me, shouldn't that be enough?'

'It would be if you didn't know more about my personal business than I'm comfortable with.' He sat back and folded his arms. 'I'll tell you what I do know. Number one, you resemble Arrosa so closely you have to be a near relative, number two, she's never mentioned you but you clearly know a lot about her life, number three, you're not Asturian, you speak the language well but there's a hint of an accent. Not French, not Spanish. If I had to bet I'd say English. So why is an English girl in Asturia pretending to be the Crown Princess?'

'I'm an actress.'

'So this is a job? All above board? Signed off by the King?'

'It's more of a private arrangement.'

'Give me one good reason why I shouldn't alert the guards to your presence here.' He didn't take his eyes off her and she knew he wasn't bluffing.

'Because I'm her half-sister,' she said. 'The family secret. And no one in Asturia is supposed to know I exist. Happy now?'

What had she just said? It took more than a few seconds for Akil's brain to process the words he'd just heard.

'You're Arrosa's half-*sister*?' He knew that the King and Queen lived largely separate lives, but he'd never heard rumours of any affairs—and certainly none of any other children. But Clem's resemblance to Arrosa was startling, sisters made perfect sense. How had this scandal been hushed

up for so long in this small country? Who
else knew?

Clem nodded. 'I'm six months older than
Rosy. Look, my existence is only known to
a very, very few people.' She looked across
at him pleadingly. 'Please don't tell anyone.
If the truth got out it would hurt Rosy more
than me. Any family scandal might rebound
on her even though she's obviously not responsible for anything apart from treating
me as much like a sister as possible. The next
few months are key, you know that. Maybe
I shouldn't have come to Asturia, maybe it
was too risky, but Rosy lives such a quiet
life outside her duties I didn't think anyone
would find out if I stuck to her villa and
slipped out to explore incognito. Shows how
much I know. I managed less than twenty-
four hours here before you found me.'

Akil sat back and sipped his coffee, his
mind racing. Clem had a point—more than
one. If news of her very existence got out
then the ensuing scandal would overshadow
the new hereditary law, and possibly disrupt
the ratification. Change came slowly to Asturia and a consensus was still very much
in the balance, as was public opinion, especially amongst the older generations. But

Clem was also right about Arrosa's need for time away. She'd looked increasingly pale and thin over the last few months and Akil knew her offer to him came from a need for companionship and help, not from any deeper feelings. Some time away was exactly what she needed—and if he hadn't turned up unexpectedly then who was to say that the ruse wouldn't have worked the way the sisters had planned it?

'I won't say a word,' he promised. 'But how is this even possible? You're six months older than Arrosa, you say, which must mean Zorien is your father? Who's your mother?' It was unlike Akil to be so overtly curious but he was intrigued beyond politeness by this secret at the very heart of the court.

Clem flushed, her eyes fixed on her cup. 'One thing you need to know is that this isn't easy for me. I have never told anyone who I am, not even my old boyfriends, or my best friend. Anyone from home who has met Rosy thinks she's my cousin. Just saying the truth aloud feels like I've broken some law.'

'You don't have to tell me anything you don't want to,' Akil assured her and her answering smile was grateful.

'I know. But in a strange way, I do want to

tell you. It's probably better that you know the whole truth rather than leaving you with just bits of it. I would hate for you to think badly of my mother, or even my father. He's not exactly been there for me, but I do understand how difficult things were for him and he has ensured that Rosy and I know each other. I will always be grateful to him for that.'

Akil did some rapid mental calculations. 'Arrosa was born a year after Zorien and Iara married—so you would have been conceived three months before?'

Clem nodded. 'What you have to remember is that Zorien's marriage was brought forward after his father's illness meant he decided to abdicate in favour of his son. There had been an informal agreement between the families that Zorien and Iara would marry but they weren't technically engaged when Zorien dated my mother. It's a bit of a technicality because the marriage was very much in the pipeline, but my father wasn't a total cad. A bit of one but not a *total* cad.' Her voice rang with sincerity. It was obviously important to her that Akil believed this—that she believed it.

Akil had never really thought about the

King's marriage before, or how it had come to be. But this was Asturian politics, nothing happened without planning for the long game, his own parents' disastrous marriage aside. 'Queen Iara comes from an old and wealthy aristocratic family with links to European royalty on both sides. I believe it was a popular marriage among the people and politically sound,' he remembered. 'And for the most part it seems to have worked well; apart from her propensity to take long retreats abroad, she's a good queen. Not loved, exactly, but respected.'

'From what I've gleaned they live mostly separate lives but put on a united front. Neither had any romantic fantasies about the marriage. Iara's family wanted her to be Queen and she liked the idea. Zorien knew his position as a young king would be stabilised by a good marriage. After the plans were agreed, but before they got engaged, Zorien was allowed to go to the Sorbonne for a year's MBA as reward. He enrolled anonymously and that's where he met my mother. They fell in love. At least, my mother told me it was love.' Her voice softened, became wistful. 'He told her the truth when his father's declining health meant the court decided to bring the engagement forward, followed by a wedding just six weeks later. What neither of them knew when they parted was that she was pregnant with me. By the time she found out the wedding was less than a month away and the abdication planned. A different man might have broken off the engagement and married my mother despite the court's objections and weathered the scandal, or even walked away from the throne altogether, but Zorien decided to put Asturia first, go ahead with the wedding and make sure no one knew about my mother or about me.'

'That must have been difficult for your mother.' And for the daughter, which made her presence here today rather remarkable. Made *her* rather remarkable. Strong, forgiving, compassionate.

Beautiful.

Desirable.

The realisation made him catch his breath. Yes, she resembled her sister, but she was very much her own person; there was a piquancy to her features that differentiated her, made her unique. Made her desirable in a way Arrosa wasn't. Not that Akil had any right to dwell on either her beauty or her desirability.

Clem's mouth twisted into a wry smile. 'My mother was a doer not a dweller.' Akil noted the *was* and the way she blinked sudden tears away at the word. 'She moved to England where I was born, fell in love with Cornwall and retrained as a teacher, although Zorien was very generous, money-wise at least. She never married, never really dated seriously as far as I know although she had plenty of suitors. Instead she threw herself into campaigns and causes, never happier than when she was directing the village play or organising a march or painting a placard. To be honest I'm not sure being a queen would have agreed with her. She liked to say exactly what was on her mind, to take action. Diplomacy wasn't really her thing.'

'How did you and Arrosa get to know each other?'

'Apparently Zorien told Iara about my mother and the pregnancy before they married. When it started to seem likely that Arrosa was going to be their only child she agreed that we should be allowed to meet. In the end Rosy used to come to us, incognito of course, for most holidays and nearly all of the summer. She loved the chance to do normal things. To go surfing or bowling, to eat chips on the beach. To get dirty and have tangled hair and old clothes. We had amazing summers. We don't get to spend time together now but we speak weekly. She's my sister, my closest friend. I love her and her happiness matters.' Her gaze was direct. 'So I am glad you and I got the chance to meet. To talk.'

Her meaning was clear. 'She told you about her proposition?'

'Yes, and that's why I urged her to stay in Cornwall. What the two of you decide is your business, but she was too tired, too run-down to make any life-altering decisions right now. I hope you will respect that she needs time and space. Her parents married for an alliance, because it made political sense, and nothing she has ever told me has persuaded me that it was a good match. I want more for her than that.'

'Understood.' He did—and he admired the way Clem had her sister's interests at heart. He'd thought Arrosa alone but how could she be with her sister on her side? He pushed his chair back. 'It was nice meeting you, Clem. Thank you for entrusting me with your secret. I promise it's safe with me. What are your plans for the next six weeks?'

She winced. 'That's a good question. I'd hoped to get to know Asturia. I've never been here before and I have always wanted to explore it. But we're miles from anywhere, Rosy doesn't own a car and the limousine isn't exactly inconspicuous. I'm not really sure how to get out and about. I can't just call a taxi when as far as anyone knows the person living here is Arrosa and never goes anywhere unaccompanied and without clearance. I'll figure out a way, but it's more complicated than I realised.'

He sympathised with her, but her predicament was none of his business. His life was complicated enough without embroiling himself in the affairs of the King's illegitimate daughter. But there was something about the wistful look in Clem's eyes and the way she tried to cover it with her cheery matter-of-fact tone that spoke to him. It *was* a shame that she couldn't get to know the country her father ruled over and her sister would one day inherit.

'I cleared my diary for the rest of the day so I could take you out this afternoon if you wanted,' he said, surprising himself with the offer. 'If you put your hair up and sunglasses on, the guards at the gate will assume you're Arrosa—I've driven her to the city before and I trained with the secret service during my national service, which means clearance has never been an issue before. The guards will assume we're working. And once we're away from here you should be fine. You don't look so like your sister that anyone would mistake you for her close up, especially if you don't dress formally.'

Hope sparked in the hazel eyes but almost immediately dimmed. 'That's very kind but I can't ask you to give up your afternoon for me.'

'You didn't ask, I offered. Your choice, Clem. A chance to explore or an afternoon staring at the lake. What will it be?' Akil didn't want to analyse why he really wanted her to say yes.

She laughed at that, the sound unexpectedly rich and melodic. 'It's not really a choice when you put it that way. Thank you, I really appreciate it and I would love to accept. Let's explore. Just give me five minutes to get ready.'

'Take as long as you need.' Akil ignored the sense of anticipation creeping through him at the prospect of an afternoon spent with the English girl, the pleasure that she had accepted his offer. He was doing a favour for his friend's sister. Nothing more, nothing less.

CHAPTER FOUR

ANTICIPATION FIZZED THROUGH Clem as she pulled on a pair of Arrosa's oversized sunglasses and added one of her sister's bright scarves and a large, low-brimmed hat. The perfect disguise as all three could be discarded as soon as she had safely left the estate grounds. She tipped her own sunglasses, phone and purse into one of Arrosa's bags and practically ran back outside.

'Ready!'

Akil was frowning at his phone but as he looked up a slow, approving smile curved his mouth and a jolt of attraction hit her low in her stomach, the heat spreading through her. 'You really were just five minutes.'

'I'm an actress, remember? Quick changes are my trade.'

'When my sister says five minutes I usually know I need to settle in for half an hour at least.'

'You have a sister?'

He nodded. 'Elixane. She's in New York at the moment, doing a surgical residency.' A shadow, so fleeting she wasn't sure if she'd imagined it, crossed his face. 'She plans to be Surgeon General here one day.'

'A woman with ambition. I approve.'

Clem quickly sent a message to Marie and Henri to let them know her plans and then followed Akil round to the front of the villa. She let out a low whistle as she took in his car. A sporty two-seater, so far so playboy but the classy silvery blue colour he'd chosen suggested a car bought to drive and enjoy as opposed to a mere status symbol. 'What a beauty! Can we have the top down?'

'If you want.'

'I do, although maybe when we're away from here and I can shed the hat. It would be a bit inconvenient if it got blown off by the wind just as we got waved through!'

Akil unlocked the car and Clem slid in, luxuriating in the comfortable leather seats. The car might seem a cliché in a less skilled driver's hands, but he handled her beautifully, the car purring under his guidance.

Clem sneaked a look at Akil as he accelerated down the drive, sunglasses shading his eyes, his face intent on the road ahead, muscles taut on his bare arms, and her pulse accelerated. He really was a ridiculously attractive man.

His arrival at the villa could so easily have been a disaster but it was looking as if it was a blessing in disguise. Not only was she finally getting an opportunity to explore Asturia, but this was an unexpected opportunity to find out who Akil really was behind the hot body and the political career, her chance to make sure he was worthy of her sister, to find out what he really thought of Arrosa's proposition.

She tensed up as they reached the gate and Akil gave her another of those slow smiles, her stomach flipping in response. 'Relax,' he said. 'You're doing fine.' Sure enough, the soldiers saluted as they opened the gates and within seconds they were accelerating away, Clem discarding the hat and sunglasses, replacing Arrosa's designer dark sunglasses with her own quirkier vintage ones and wriggling back in her seat.

'Where are we going?'

'I can tell you,' Akil said. 'Or it could be a surprise. Your call.'

Everywhere was new to her and she wanted to see it all. 'I trust you. Surprise me. I'm sure anywhere you choose will be fine.'

Akil nodded as he pressed the button to lower the roof and the whistle of the wind combined with the purr of the engine. Clem stared around at the countryside, taking it all in with avid eyes. She'd seen so many pictures, read so many books, watched any programme or film set here and now she was actually here, breathing Asturian air.

Asturia was as beautiful as she had hoped, green and unspoilt with verges filled with wild flowers. Her very soul felt repleted as she inhaled the tartly fresh air as if something in her had always craved it. As if she were home. Asturia might be backward in many ways but that meant its countryside was relatively undeveloped and the country was now getting a reputation for biodiversity and attracting eco-conscious tourists. Rolling hills and fields gave way to mountains at the further end of the horizon, the sun beating down from a cloudless sky. She sighed in appreciation. 'It's so beautiful.'

'It really is,' Akil agreed. 'There's no-where else like it.'

'And so quiet. As if there's no one else here.'

'Hmm.' He glanced in the mirror. 'Apart from the car that's been tailing us since we left the castle. Is Henri not with Arrosa? I thought he never left her side?'

She looked round at the sleek black car hanging a discreet distance behind. 'Poor Henri. He was torn between returning with me and staying with Rosy. As people are meant to think I'm her he knew he needed to be here for business as usual, but he takes protecting her very seriously. It took some persuading for him to agree that she'd look too conspicuous if he stayed. No one expects my cousin to have a bodyguard! Although I expect Zorien has dispatched someone to keep an eye on her.'

'Your father knows you've swapped?'

'Rosy messaged him last night. I was hop-ing to hear from him today but of course he's very busy. This would be such a good opportunity for us to spend some time to-gether.' She could hear the self-pity in her voice and winced, relieved when Akil didn't pursue the subject.

They crested a hill and as they reached
the top and the sea came into view Clem
gasped. There it was, laid out before them,
turquoise and silver and so dazzling she was
glad of her sunglasses. She took in a wondering breath as Akil began to navigate his
way down the curving road.

'It's like something out of a fairy tale,'
she said softly, transfixed as the flower-
covered cliffs came into view, the sea tumbling against them. Asturia wasn't the most
famous of tourist resorts, but there was no
coastline to rival it, not even her beloved
Cornwall. 'Just like I imagined,' she almost
whispered.

They carried on heading along the coast
road until Akil turned off down a narrow
lane, heading towards the sea and a tiny
cluster of houses dotted around a wooden,
slightly tatty harbour. Clem knew that there
were plenty of glamorous beaches along the
coast, home to exclusive beach clubs and
harbours filled with fancy boats, but this
seemed like the kind of place she loved,
small and known only to a few locals.

Akil pulled into a car park and killed the
engine. Clem looked around eagerly. Fishing boats bobbed by the wooden pier, bigger

boats moored further out, a mix of working and leisure craft. In front of them a small hut overlooked the sea flanked by a few plastic tables and chairs.

'Okay, then,' he said. 'Here we are. I hope you're hungry.'

It was as if Akil had seen inside her soul and knew exactly what she craved. She followed him to the hut and took a seat on a battered but clean and comfortable plastic chair perched on the edge of a tiny stone harbour, fine white sand inviting her on the beach to their right.

'What do you fancy?' Akil asked. 'I can recommend the fried clams.'

'Clams and fries? Perfect.'

'The local beer is good, or they make their own lemonade.'

'A beer sounds good. In a way I am on holiday, I suppose.' Not that she'd been gainfully employed for longer than she cared to remember. Money wasn't an issue, thanks to the money Zorien had set aside for her, but she needed an occupation. She needed a purpose, a reason to exist. She pushed the thought away for another day and tilted her chin. 'Besides, this is my first outing in Asturia. I should celebrate.'

Akil held her gaze for one charged second, the corner of his mouth turned up in amusement—and approval. Clem's pulse thudded under his studied gaze and she turned to exclaim at the view, breaking the spell with a stream of meaningless words.

The food was as wonderful as promised, the clams fat and salty, tasting like the sea, the fries crispy on the outside, meltingly soft inside, tart with vinegar. The salad wasn't the token collection of browned limp leaves Clem was expecting, but sweet crunchy leaves, tiny, delicious tomatoes and tart red peppers, another reminder that she was in the Mediterranean, not on the English coast.

Even better was the view. On one side the sea, calm and bright and endlessly beautiful, and on the other Akil. Six feet of broad-shouldered, olive-skinned, dark-eyed deliciousness. And she *really* needed to stop thinking about Akil that way. She wasn't here on a date. She didn't know him, nor he her. He was just being kind to a lonely girl. And no doubt it suited him to do it. He must know that Clem would tell Arrosa all about the afternoon.

But she couldn't deny that this really was her idea of a dream date. And that spelt trouble in all kinds of ways she wasn't going to allow herself to think about.

Instead, she was going to keep busy and push the words *dream* and *date* right out of her mind.

'That was amazing,' she said, jumping to her feet and collecting up the plates and beer bottles and returning them to the hut with a smile. 'Thank you for bringing me here.' She didn't return to her seat, leaning over the railing and looking out to sea, her pulse hammering with nerves. *Keep talking, Clem.* She glanced back at Akil. 'So this is a favourite place of yours?'

'Since I was a boy,' he confirmed, lounging back in his chair. 'My aunt has a holiday home near here, me, my sister and our cousins spent our summers sailing on these waters and spending all our money on snacks here at this very shack. Not that it spoiled our appetites.' His grin was reminiscently boyish and her stomach tumbled. She could cope with him being handsome. She wasn't sure she could manage charming as well.

'I was brought up by the sea. I love sailing. Surfing, paddle-boarding, kayaking, I did it all. I just love being out on the water.'

'It can be arranged, just say the word. My boat is moored here.'

He had a boat? Could he tick any more boxes? Regretfully she shook her head. 'I can't let poor Henri follow us in a dinghy.' She grimaced. 'I'd never realised how limiting it is being followed all the time. I know that Henri is kind, careful not to impose, but he's always there. I don't know how Rosy manages it.'

'What she has now is freedom compared to how her life will be once she's the heir to the throne.'

It was a sobering thought. No wonder her sister wanted companionship. Two sisters equally lonely but for very different reasons. Maybe Rosy should marry Akil. He was kind, intelligent and understood her world.

But then again she didn't love him and, of all people, didn't her sister deserve love?

'Maybe I should stick around and be her body double for good and then she could escape whenever she needed,' she half joked and Akil grinned.

'Maybe you should. Although poor Henri would definitely want to clone himself if you two made a habit of this.' He nodded towards the beach. 'Fancy walking some of that off?'

'Absolutely. I'm dying to explore.'

The beach was a long straight strip of white sand, the sea lapping at the edges. In the distance Clem could see a gentle curve and a high tumble of rocks against the high cliff that marked the end of the bay. They started to walk, first slowly and then faster as they took the measure of each other's stride, and Clem enjoyed the pace, the stretch in her muscles as she matched Akil step for step. She could hear the occasional hum of a car, the screech of gulls out at sea, but otherwise it was as if it were just the two of them—and Henri, several hundred yards behind.

Neither spoke, their strides perfectly matched. Clem was totally aware of Akil's every movement, the swing of his arms, the flex of his hands. She swallowed, trying to ignore the all-encompassing awareness of him that seemed to grow with every passing minute. *Behave*, she scolded herself, aware that she needed to stop staring at his wrists, stop finding herself transfixed by the pulse at his throat, stop dwelling on the lines of his mouth, stop allowing herself to trace the outlines of his strong, broad body.

It was just attraction, but it was inconvenient and misjudged.

'Are you seriously considering it?' she asked abruptly. 'Rosy's idea?'

Akil's brows drew together in surprise, a haughty expression crossing his face, and she winced at her gaucheness, scrambling to explain. 'I meant what I said earlier, it's your decision and not really my business. But in some ways it *is*. I've spent just a few hours in my sister's shoes and I can see why she feels she needs someone permanent on her side, in her team. It's pretty lonely being a princess. But I still think rushing into an engagement, into a marriage, is just a temporary fix. Because if you're not right for each other she'll end up lonelier than before. I love her,' she said awkwardly. 'And I hate that I can't support her the way a sister should. So maybe I'm interfering but I can't just pretend that this situation isn't worrying me.'

Akil's face softened as she spoke. 'My parents are the perfect example of a hasty ill-thought-out marriage so please be assured I would never rush into any kind of decision. My father was an ambitious man, my mother a country girl. Theirs was a summer romance which should have stayed a lovely memory but instead became an unhappy marriage.'

'That sounds tough. They're still together?'

'Legally, but in reality they see very little of each other. My mother resides at the family home, my father retired after a heart attack eight years ago and now lives mainly in Switzerland.' A heart attack Akil had been responsible for. He could never forget that.

'What happened?'

He didn't answer for a while, instead he paused and turned, his gaze far away on the horizon. 'My mother understood little of politics and hated my father's absences,' he said at last. 'She didn't want a husband who spent most of his time away from home, whereas he wanted a hostess to work the room, someone to charm allies and rivals and know all the gossip, not a shy, paranoid wife who drank too much to work up the courage to have a conversation. They were very different, too different. They made each other unhappy, everyone around them unhappy. With different partners, in another life, they might have been better people, happier people, but we'll never know. If I marry, then I know to look for shared goals, compatibility, not momentary attraction.'

'And love? Do you want love?'

'Love can complicate things. It's not essential for me. Liking and respect mean more to me than love.'

She nodded. 'Thank you for your honesty.'

'And?'

'And what?'

'Did I pass?'

It was her turn to pause and think, to search for the right words. 'I like your honesty and self-awareness and I like the fact that you understand my sister's world and aren't intimidated by it. But I still think she should wait for someone who loves her, not her job, someone who would marry her if she ran the shack on the beach or cleaned her office. And we both know that's not you. But,' she added hurriedly, aware she was interfering in a way she had promised herself not to, 'this isn't about what I think. You two have to decide what's best for you. But can I ask you something?'

'Anything. It doesn't mean I'll answer but you can ask.'

'What's in it for you? You don't strike me as the kind of man who likes to play second fiddle, and I know what a macho culture Asturia has. Do you really see yourself as a consort?'

Akil was floored by Clem's directness, by her honesty. Floored—and intrigued and more than a little impressed. It was so far from the kind of language used in the Senate and at Court, no dancing around, no double-speak. Instead she aimed straight for the heart of the matter and hit it.

'Power,' he said simply. 'If I marry your sister, if I became Prince Consort, then I will always be at the very heart of policy, of government, a decision maker, and influencer.'

Her brow furrowed. 'And that matters to you?'

He laughed shortly. 'I'm a politician. Power is all that matters, Clem.'

'Power for power's sake?'

He hated the uncertainty in her voice. 'No, but without power nothing can be achieved. My family has been at the heart of government for generations, carrying on their work is my destiny whether I like it or not. I haven't always agreed, but when my father had his heart attack and had to take early retirement I promised him that I would fulfil his dreams. That promise means a lot to me. But, as I said, I know the pitfalls of marrying rashly and wrongly. I could achieve great things in my current role too. I just need to weigh it all up.'

'You're close to your father?' He could hear the wistfulness in her voice as she asked the question and winced.

'I wouldn't say close,' he said wryly. 'I don't think anyone is. My father is…very single-minded. He sees no views but his own, brooks no opinion but his own. He's not an easy man.'

'But he must be proud of you,' she argued. 'Rosy said that you are the youngest, most influential politician in Asturia. And look at your sister, a surgeon in New York. Surely that success means a lot to him?'

'The only thing that would make my father proud is if my sister marries someone he approves of and if I keep climbing the political ladder. Would he approve of me marrying your sister? Without a doubt. Does that influence me? It shouldn't, but…' he shrugged '…I can't deny that his approval is something I seek. Maybe it's a weakness.' He strode on, appalled at how much he'd said, how much he'd revealed, how much he'd exposed. It wasn't like him to speak about his family, about his own insecurities and complicated feelings around his father's push for Akil to do more, to be more. What was it about this woman that made him speak without fear or thought?

He sensed Clem catch up beside him and they walked along in silence for a little longer. 'I understand better than you know,' she said at last, her voice quiet. 'I've only met my father a handful of times, he's never seen me act, never said well done after an exam result, he wasn't there the day I buried my mother. I should hate him, sometimes I do, but more than anything I want him to notice me, want him to be proud of me. I want him to acknowledge I exist.'

Akil didn't know what to say, so instead of words he reached out and took her hand. It was warm in his, fitted him as if made for him to hold. 'I'm sure he knows. He's like my father, not a man to show his emotions.' Akil reluctantly dropped her hand, his own instantly cold.

'True, but knowing it's not personal doesn't make it any easier. I hate that I care. I'm twenty-seven, a grown woman. I shouldn't let the way I feel about him affect my life. But it does. Sometimes I think the only reason I became an actress was to be seen. For the moment the applause rings out for me and I relish the validation that gives me. Pathetic, isn't it?' She shook her head, her mouth compressed tight.

'Not at all,' he said softly. 'We all need validation. What about your mother? Did you have a good relationship with her?'

Clem stared down at the sand, digging into it with her trainer toes. 'I did, we were very close, and I miss her every day. But my mother, she was a force of nature. Not many women would take in their ex-lover's daughter every summer, but my mother loved every waif and stray. Every cat we owned was a runaway she ended up feeding. She was a woman who embraced causes, was at the heart of every campaign, her life was big and filled and sometimes it felt like there was little room for me. Everything was open to anyone who needed it, from Christmases to time together. She just had this endless capacity to scoop people up and look after them, but it meant I always had to share her.' She gave a little laugh. 'I know that I sound so selfish, so spoiled. But sometimes I just wanted to be first with one of my parents just once. If I ever marry, if I ever have kids, it will be different. Maybe it's boring, but I want the house and garden and the kids playing on the trampoline and a husband who loves me. Who sees me. And I want that for Rosy too, because she needs it just as much, more in some ways.'

Akil turned to face her. 'Are you warning me off?'

'No.' She shook her head. 'Not at all. And I'll tell Rosy all about this conversation. I just want you to know that there's more to her than the practical Princess and I bet there's more to you than the ambitious politician and you both need to take that into consideration.'

'I will,' he vowed, and he meant it. 'Come on, I'd better get you back.'

'Have I frightened you off?'

He laughed at that. 'No. In fact you've intrigued me. I'm glad I met you today, Clem. I can't help thinking that in another time, another place, we might have been friends.'

That was only partly true, because in another time and another place he would have liked to have known her a lot better, to have explored the attraction he could feel building between them.

'Friends?' she echoed. 'Yes, I would have liked that. Thank you for today, Akil. Not just for the trip and the food, but for listening.'

'Any time.' And he meant it. It was just a shame their paths were unlikely to cross again.

CHAPTER FIVE

HEART POUNDING, LEGS ACHING, Akil reached his apartment door, opened it and staggered in to collapse on the sofa, his water bottle within reach. Ten miles in the heat of the early afternoon at that pace had been foolish but he'd needed the exercise.

Needed to get Clem out of his mind.

It had been *one* meeting. One afternoon. Just a few hours spent together. But somehow in those hours he'd been more honest with her than he had been with any other human being for years—including himself. He couldn't hide from the question she'd asked him. Instead it swirled throughout his mind relentlessly.

What was in it for him if he married Arrosa?

The answers came quickly and glibly. The same answers he'd given her: power, the ability to get things done, a place at the heart of all decision-making, marriage to someone compatible without any of the emotions or passions that could so easily turn dark and disrupt the equilibrium he craved. And most importantly of all, a chance to show his father that he was not only a true Ortiz, but he was better than him, had achieved more, to not just keep his promise, but to surpass it. Surpass him.

To show himself that giving up his own dreams had been worth it. Arrosa would never have made the suggestion if he'd become a doctor, no matter how skilled or successful he might have been.

Akil sank onto the sofa. They were all compelling reasons, but no matter how often he repeated them he couldn't make them ring true. He liked Arrosa, respected her, but he couldn't imagine spending a lifetime with her. Couldn't imagine treading someone else's path, not again. He'd already compromised his life's purpose once and had vowed never again.

And there were other reasons to refuse, as compelling as those in favour. The Ortizes were an old family but not known outside Asturia. Whoever married Arrosa would be instantly targeted by the world's press. Look what that meant for the royal family, even the unacknowledged daughter: Clem never having the opportunity to build a real relationship with her father, Arrosa resorting to subterfuge to get time alone, bodyguards always around. It wouldn't take much digging to uncover the truth about his family, about his mother's drinking and his father's affairs. There was no way Akil wanted their dirty laundry spread all over the Internet.

At that moment his phone rang and Akil reached for it, only mildly surprised when he saw the Princess's name flash up. She'd messaged him yesterday in reply to his question checking in on her, but of course she'd have had the opportunity to speak to Clem since then. The question was, what had Clem said about their time together? Would the Princess want to pursue her idea or was this call to let him down?

Either way his mind was made up.

'Your Highness, you're alive,' he said as he answered it. 'I have to say it comes as some relief. I've been hoping that I wasn't taken in by a very clever con artist.'

Arrosa laughed, sounding far more relaxed than he'd ever heard her sound before.

'Clem is definitely good enough an actress to be a con artist, but she's far too straight talking.'

Akil smiled wryly. 'I noticed that myself.'

'Yes, I bet you did. She gave me a very interesting account of your conversation. I'm not going to apologise, it's nice to know that someone is looking out for me, but I hope it wasn't too bruising.'

'Bracing maybe, but not bruising. She certainly made me think.'

A trace of caution entered Arrosa's voice. 'She's good at that. That's why she insisted that I take some time away, to give *me* time to look at what I really want for my future. And I have. I know I've only been gone a couple of days but being away from Asturia, away from the court, away from all the pressure and hysteria around the ratification, has been exactly what I needed.'

She paused and he heard her inhale. 'Look, Akil, I think I owe you an apology…'

And there it was, his get-out-of-becoming-royalty card. The relief that filled him was surprisingly overwhelming. 'You don't need to say anything,' he said. 'Let's just pretend that the end of that last conversation never happened.'

'I shouldn't have said anything. I was tired and honestly a little scared of what's happening this year…'

'Listen, I'm flattered, but Clem's right. You deserve more.'

'She said that?'

'And the rest. Arrosa, I hope it goes without saying that I will continue to do all I can to support you, and I hope we can work together for many years. More than that, I hope that we can become friends, real friends.'

'I'd like that. Friends sounds good.'

'In that case, Arrosa, as your friend, can I ask if you're okay?'

She paused again and when she spoke her voice broke a little. 'Yes, in some ways I'm more okay than I have been for a long time. And with Clem covering for me I'm perfectly safe. Life in Asturia can be very suffocating. I am appreciating having the chance to breathe.'

'That's good.'

'It really is. Although I feel guilty that Clem must now be feeling hemmed in, especially as she can't really go out and meet people. So thank you for taking her out, for giving her a chance to see something of the country. I really appreciate it.'

It seemed wrong to be thanked for one of the most enjoyable afternoons he'd had in a long time. 'You don't need to thank me. Your sister's an interesting woman. I enjoyed her company very much—and it strikes me that she knows exactly what she signed up for and is determined to see it through.'

'I offered to swap back, but she won't hear of it.' The relief in Arrosa's voice was palpable; no wonder Clem had insisted on maintaining the charade a little bit longer. Admiration for the Englishwoman filled him. He knew it wasn't easy for her trapped alone in the villa, no matter how beautiful the outlook and luxurious the furnishings.

'I think she's made up her mind to make sure you get a good long break. It's an honourable thing she's doing. She has integrity.'

'She's the best sister I could have. I just wish I could tell the whole world who she is, that she could be part of my life openly. I hope she's not too bored. I know she won't tell me if she is. Life at the estate can be confining, even though I insisted on moving out of the palais into the lake house, and of course she doesn't have work to keep her occupied. She says she's fine and it's a change of scene, but six weeks is a long time to be stuck in one place and alone.'

'I could pop in and check on her, if you want.' Akil's tone was nonchalant but he could feel his pulse speed up at the thought.

'That would be really kind. I would really appreciate it.' Was that amusement in Arrosa's voice?

'I'll see if I can spare the time.'

'Thank you, Akil. For everything.'

'Enjoy your break.' As Akil ended the call he couldn't shake the feeling that he'd been set up in some way.

Maybe checking on Clem wasn't such a good idea. He couldn't deny that he was attracted to her, was intrigued by her, but she was only here for a short while and he had too much going on to invite the kind of complications she posed further into his life. Better to leave her as a memorable momentary encounter.

It was definitely safer and wiser that way.

But he couldn't help wishing that she had been someone else.

For the next few days Akil kept himself too busy to dwell on might-have-beens and if-onlys. It was the parliamentary summer recess and, although there were always briefing notes to read and events to react to, it gave him more time to do the things he truly loved. His dream of being a doctor might have died the day his father had collapsed with a heart attack, but his desire to help, be part of and reform the creaky, unequal health system in Asturia hadn't and he had undertaken mountain rescue training and now volunteered whenever he could. It wasn't what he'd once hoped for, but it was better than nothing and the insight the volunteering gave him helped him push for the reforms the country needed. Even his father approved— a politician who got involved with mountain rescue played well in the polls. Now it was early summer there were plenty of inexperienced hikers walking Asturia's famous mountain trails spraining ankles and getting lost and Akil could easily spend twelve hours a day either coordinating searches or out himself. By the time he got in most evenings he was no good for anything but feeding his cat, grabbing a beer and a sandwich and collapsing on the sofa.

One night he had ended up being called out late to help locate a missing couple who had gone out to look at the stars and not returned and it was the early hours before he got back in. Too wired to sleep, he didn't get to bed until it was almost dawn, sleeping in until noon, almost unheard of with his busy schedule. Looking around, he realised the toll the last few days had taken: he had little food in and his usually neat apartment felt both untidy and unlived in, his cat grumpy and aloof as if indignant at being left alone for so long.

After toasting the end of the loaf and whisking up his last two eggs, he sank onto the sofa and switched on the TV to catch the news. His counterpart had made an announcement about a new security law, and although Akil had read some of the online reactions he was interested to see what the state TV news would say. It was the lead item, and once it was finished he fumbled for the remote to switch over to the sports channel when the sight of a familiar profile made him pause.

To any casual onlooker the profile through the tinted window looked enough like Arrosa for there to be no doubt that this was the Princess being driven back to her home from the capital city. Huge sunglasses shielded most of her face, but the features were familiar, her hair was up in the kind of complicated knot Arrosa favoured and her posture and half-smile were so like Arrosa's own he'd have been fooled himself if he hadn't known better. Warmth filled him as he watched the brief clip of Clem doing what she'd come here to do: fool the press into thinking Arrosa was safe in Asturia.

Warmth that soon faded as he remembered his unfulfilled promise. What had she been doing for the last four days? Had her father come to see her? He doubted it. She was probably all alone.

But she shouldn't be because he'd promised Arrosa he'd look in on her and, unlike many other politicians, he prided himself on keeping his promises. It was wrong of him to stay away just because he was attracted to her—after all, he'd been attracted to lots of women in his life and been perfectly capable of spending time with them.

Before he could think better of it, he quickly texted Arrosa and asked for Clem's number. The reply came back lightning quick, as if Arrosa had been waiting for the question. Akil saved the number and sent a quick exploratory message. There, it was up to her now. He didn't mind either way.

So why was he checking his phone to see the message had been read?

'I'm a fool, Tiger,' he said to his cat, who as usual ignored him. But just as he put his phone out of reach, determined to concentrate on the game, his phone pinged.

His pulse sped as he reached for the phone and checked the name of the sender. Clem. She'd replied. His finger hovered over her name; it shouldn't matter if she gave him a polite brush off or an acceptance, but Akil couldn't deny the thrill of anticipation as he contemplated the message.

Nor could he deny how much he hoped her answer was a yes.

Clem was doing her best to put a Pollyanna spin on her experience. Number one: the weather was beautiful and her tan was coming along nicely. Number two: Arrosa's villa was luxuriously and comfortably furnished with everything she could need and more besides, including some seriously luxurious toiletries, which turned every day into a spa day. Number three: she had the lake at her disposal. The small rowing boat in the boathouse was perfect for spending a couple of hours sculling up and down the lake in, and the water, although cold, was clean and clear enough for some serious swimming. She had got into the habit of taking both a morning dip and sunset swim and on a hot day could be found spending most of the afternoon in the water as well. She just hoped this behaviour wasn't so out of character that it was raising eyebrows amongst bodyguards and staff who saw her from afar. Number four: there was a castle kitchen at her disposal. All she had to do was order her food and it turned up, like magic in her kitchen although she'd never seen anyone bring it over or put it out for her. Even when she didn't order anything the kitchen was mysteriously stocked in her absence, freshly made bread, cream butter, sharp cheese, olives and delicious little cakes replenishing themselves or so it seemed. Her sister might live independently, but she definitely had all the perks of living at home. Her laundry disappeared too, only to return clean and pressed.

And, last but not least, she had the time she needed to think about her future. Time away from Cornwall and the memories of her mother. Time to ready herself to move on to whatever the next stage of her life entailed.

But even Clem at her most determined couldn't be Pollyanna all the time, and when she stopped the reality of her situation came crashing down on her. She had been here nearly a week and her father still hadn't found time to come and see her. She wasn't so naive as to expect him to drop everything and rush over straight away, although that would have been nice, but she had hoped that now she was just a half-hour drive away he might have been able to carve out a little bit of time to see her. *Idiot*, she scolded herself. She should have known better than to expect anything from him. He'd made sure she was materially provided for and that was all she realistically could and should expect.

Plus, although she'd told herself that what she needed was time away, it turned out you really could have too much of a good thing. Her days seemed endless and her mind was whirling with possibilities and fears. It seemed impossible that less than two years ago she had been sharing a flat with friends in Battersea, filling her days with classes and auditions and sometimes even work, her evenings with bars and restaurants and plays. She'd never doubted that she would make it, that her talent and drive weren't enough. It was just a matter of when her break would be, not if.

But then she'd received the call from her mother and all that fell away, her life became a worried regime of hospital appointments and waiting rooms, too brief moments of hope and long days of bitter grief, watching her home turn slowly into a hospice for those last long, painful months.

For the three months after the packed-out funeral she had been numb with grief, wandering along the beach, curling up in her mother's bed, until the opportunity to play Juliet and the possibility of the theatre's privatisation had galvanised her back into some kind of action and routine. She'd joined the Save Our Theatre campaign, aware of just how proud her mother would have been, attending planning meetings and organising petitions, turning the cottage into a campaign headquarters just as it had been throughout her life. But although both had filled her thoughts and hours, neither were a solution to the question of what came next. In the end she'd followed her sister's advice and written a list of possibilities along with pros and cons and scores out of ten for how each one inspired her. It was time to revisit it.

Almost reluctantly she brought up the file on her tablet and set it before her on the outside table. She had a fresh coffee and a bowl of mixed fruit so she couldn't distract herself with a trip to the kitchen. Taking a deep breath, Clem read through the short list.

First and most obvious: acting. Not only had she trained for it, but she still had an agent somehow, despite her long break. Plus, she'd loved playing Juliet and was enjoying impersonating her sister and getting into character as the Crown Princess, even if it was for just an hour sitting in a car. But she knew that at some point in the last eighteen months she'd lost the resilience she needed to face the constant rejection that awaited every aspiring actor. Did she really want the high point of her month to be a recall for a toothpaste ad? Did she want to spend another three months as an understudy, sitting in the dressing room every night trying not to wish a broken ankle on the star? At twenty-five that had just been part and parcel of the process, but at twenty-seven she needed more than constant knock-backs and waiting around for her break.

Secondly, and maybe even more obviously, she could follow so many of her drama school friends into teaching. Clem sighed. It was a worthy career and her mother, with her zeal and passion for change, had been a wonderful teacher. But she didn't feel a vocation and surely that was important?

Or she could carry on putting off making a decision and go travelling, hoping she would find her vocation as she did so. After all, her mother had backpacked around the world more than once before enrolling at the Sorbonne. She had been full of stories of the time she had worked in a school in Ecuador or had crewed on a Greenpeace ship. Simone Beaumont, trying to save the world even as a backpacker. She'd always encouraged Clem to follow her example and why not? It wasn't as if she didn't have the money and the time. But she didn't want to do it alone.

She didn't want to do any of it alone, not any more. She wanted people of her own to live and laugh and love with. That was what mattered to her. That was what she needed.

But that wasn't something she could just make happen.

Clem sat back and rubbed her eyes. 'Get over yourself, Beaumont,' she muttered. 'You are luckier than so many other people. You have a home and you don't need to worry about money, you have qualifications and prospects even if you're not sure what they are yet. Stop feeling sorry for yourself. What would Maman say?'

Simone Beaumont had had no time for self-pity.

Her phone pinged and, glad of the distraction, she picked up her phone to look at the notification—an unknown number.

'Ooh, what kind of spam will it be? An uncollected parcel or a tax rebate? Or maybe it's not spam but a producer hearing about how devastating I was as Juliet and wanting me in the West End.'

She missed her mother's cat. Talking out loud didn't feel as foolish when she was addressing Gus, who always seemed on the verge of saying something wise.

She clicked it open, unprepared for the thrill of anticipation that ran through her when she saw who it was from.

Akil.

It had been five days since their lunch. After their parting she'd not expected to hear from him again, although a tiny part of her had hoped to be proved wrong, especially once Arrosa had told her that they

had decided to remain just friends and colleagues after all. But after a couple of days
had passed with no word from him, she'd
done her best to put him out of her mind.
Now here he was. What did he want?

The message was short and to the point.

If you're still finding it hard to play tourist, I
have a spare afternoon tomorrow. Shall I pick
you up? Let me know. Akil

Clem sat back, unable to stop a small
smile playing on her mouth. The part of
her that had stopped knowing how to enjoy
life over the last eighteen months, the part
of her that knew that sometimes the worst
did happen, advised caution. But the part
of her that had propelled her here, that acknowledged how very attractive she found
Akil—and was all too aware that Akil was
now unattached—urged her towards acceptance. Without stopping to think she pressed
reply and quickly typed.

That sounds great. I'm due another trip out
as Arrosa, so why don't I get Henri to take me
somewhere where I can do a quick change
afterwards and then meet you at your apart-

ment? Send me your address and let me know what time. Thanks so much. Clem

She read it over quickly, and then before she lost her nerve she pressed send. Excitement and nerves warred but she pushed both back. It was an afternoon out, nothing more, nothing less. She deserved some fun.

Clem did her best to return her attention to the list, but right now the future seemed far away. Tomorrow she was going sightseeing with an attractive man. That was good enough for now.

CHAPTER SIX

AKIL STRODE ACROSS his apartment to pick out a different shirt and realised that he was whistling. Again.

Actually, he'd been whistling all morning. He'd even sung in the shower and it was a long time since he'd done that. Not since he'd accepted his role as a politician in fact. Yet here he was. Whistling and deliberating over his outfit. As if he were fifteen again and arranging to meet a girl on a beach.

At least his hands weren't clammy, and he'd learned not to gel his hair in the last fifteen years. But maybe he should channel that boy and lose the suit. It was a little over the top for an afternoon sightseeing. He checked his watch. Clem would be here soon so if he was going to change he'd better do it now. He didn't want to greet her half naked.

He'd just finished changing when his

buzzer sounded and he strolled across to the videocam and pressed the button but, instead of Clem, Henri, suited and stern, filled the small screen.

'Subject ready. All clear?' Henri barked and Akil resisted the urge to salute.

'Everything's fine, send her up,' he said easily and pressed the button, opening the front door.

Akil waited by the open door, trying to ignore his heart hammering with anticipation. Light footsteps tripped up the stairs and there she was at his door, dressed like the tourist she was rather than the Crown Princess she'd pretended to be earlier that day, in a pretty vintage-style green sundress teamed with a denim jacket and trainers, and white sunglasses, her hair cascading loose and wild.

She looked utterly beautiful.

'Hi,' he said, mouth dry.

'Hi.' She hovered on the other side of the door, and he stood back.

'You found it okay? No problem getting here without anyone thinking you were your sister?'

'All good thanks to Henri,' she said. 'I did a quick change in a secret underground car park he knows and then he brought me here in a different car. I feel like a glamorous spy!'

'Where is he?'

'Lurking outside in case anyone followed us. Obviously a high level of paranoia is part of all bodyguard training.'

'A prerequisite,' he agreed. 'Ah, do you want to come in?'

'I thought you'd never ask.' Her hazel eyes gleamed, more green than brown today, thanks to the vibrancy of her dress. She stepped inside and glanced around. 'So this is where Asturia's most promising young politician lives?'

'It's where *I* live.' Akil tried to see his home through her eyes. His apartment was in a medieval building, all thick stone walls and tall arched windows. The floor gleamed honey brown, the old wood polished to a shine and covered by antique faded rugs. The walls were exposed stone, bookcases lining one wall, filled with books picked up over the years. Faded brown leather sofas grouped around the fireplace, one occupied by a fat ginger cat. Arrosa gave a little cry of delight and went straight over to rub its head.

'You have a *cat*?' She couldn't have

sounded more incredulous if he'd had a panther in his apartment.

'You're not allergic?'

'No, I love cats. What's his name?'

'How do you know it's a he?'

'Ginger cats usually are.' She smiled as the cat rolled over to expose a fluffy white tummy. 'Oh, aren't you handsome? Name?'

'Tiger.' Akil tried not to grimace as she unsuccessfully tried to hide a smile.

'Oh, very original.'

'I didn't name him.'

'Really.' She gave him a disbelieving look. 'Who did?'

'A neighbour's kid. Tiger belongs to them really but they had to move abroad and couldn't take him so I said I would look after him.'

'So a cat man not a dog man. Interesting!'

'I wouldn't say that. But I live in an apartment, I work a lot. It wouldn't be fair on a dog. You?'

'I like both.'

'Very diplomatic.'

'And true. We always had cats growing up. Maman said we were too busy for a dog, it wouldn't be fair. But one day I will have one—and several cats too.' She scratched the top of Tiger's head again and the feline tilted his head up, eyes half closed, purring under the caresses. Akil felt a stab of something that felt remarkably and absurdly like jealousy.

'Come on, I'll show you the rest.'

It didn't take long to show her the open-plan kitchen and dining room and the small second bedroom he used as an office. They didn't go into his bedroom; it felt too intimate. Instead he swung the door open to show her the neat room, and he just indicated the bathroom. Clem noted every detail, asking about the photographs and paintings he'd chosen, lingering over his books and greeting them like old friends.

'I like your apartment,' she said, leafing through a poetry anthology. 'But it's not what I expected.'

'What did you expect?'

'Something to match your car, all modern and sleek and styled. This…' She waved a hand. 'This feels like a home.'

'Thank you.' He tried for light, but he was surprisingly touched by her words. 'I think so too.'

'So what's the plan?'

'We're going to be tourists in the city. I

hope you're wearing sturdy shoes. We have a lot of ground to cover.'

She didn't answer for a long moment, anxiety creasing her forehead, and he looked enquiringly at her.

'The city?' she said at last. 'That's pretty busy. Is it safe?'

'Asturia's one of the safest countries in the world.'

'I mean for me, for you, for us to be seen together? Won't people wonder who you're with? You're not exactly unknown and in my experience young, single, prominent men attract attention, especially when accompanied by women.'

'The Asturian press is a lot more respectful of private lives than most of the European press and most people aren't interested in what politicians do in their own time as long as they're not obviously corrupt. If I took you to an official event or we were seen together at the races or a regatta or some other society occasion, then we would expect to be photographed and questions asked, but not if we're just walking around the city. And although you look a lot like your sister, you're not so alike that anyone would seriously mistake you for her, especially when you dress so casually. We're safe.'

She exhaled and he saw her visibly relax. 'Okay, that's reassuring. In that case what are we waiting for?'

'You to stop reading poetry.'

She closed the book and carefully reshelved it. 'Done! Come on, then, let's go.'

'After you.' He held the door open for her to precede him out and closed it behind him, realising how much he was looking forward to the afternoon. To spending time with Clem, to showing her the city he loved. This might only be their second meeting but he was already comfortable with her in a way that was unusual for Akil. His family, his position, his own natural reserve created barriers between him and most people, but somehow Clem had effortlessly battered them aside without him even noticing. This afternoon was supposed to be a favour for Arrosa, a day out for Clem, but it was turning into an unexpected treat for him too.

Clem broke into a skip as she walked through the busy streets at Akil's side, relieved to be out and about, surrounded by people like a normal person once again. Akil was right, nobody gave them a second look, even though Akil still cut an imposing figure dressed down in jeans and a T-shirt.

Although maybe he was *especially* imposing dressed down in jeans and a T-shirt. The grey T-shirt was faded, clearly well worn, but it looked as if it had been expensive, well cut and fitted, clinging to toned arms and showing off the breadth of his chest and shoulders, the flatness of his stomach. His jeans were perfectly cut, riding low on narrow hips and showcasing what she couldn't help but notice was a very nice butt—she was only human after all—and clinging to muscled thighs.

The sun shone, a perfect Mediterranean mid June day, and she was glad of her sunglasses as it bounced and sparkled off the paved streets, marble pavements and shop windows as she eagerly looked around, drinking in every sight, sound and smell.

The Asturian capital city, Asturia Valle, was a medieval city set in a large valley and ringed by the mountains that made up the bulk of the small country. Beautiful as the coastline was, it was the mountains that lured the tourists in, skiers in winter, walkers in summer, the blue lakes that dotted the valleys and mountain shelfs a magnet for skaters, swimmers and water sports enthusiasts.

Clem wanted to explore every inch of her country. And this was the perfect start. Akil knew exactly where he was going, steering her to one of the tourist booths dotted around the city, where he left her for a couple of minutes, reappearing with a map and a couple of tickets.

'I've got us these,' he said, handing her one of the tickets.

Clem squinted at it as she made out the small printed words. 'A one-day city pass?'

'This gets us in everywhere.'

'Everywhere?'

'The castle, the city museum, the zoo, the cable car, the funicular railway, the steam railway, the cathedral, the walking tours, all five of them, discounts at the theatre and the opera house and several restaurants and cafes. Pretty much everywhere.' His smile was smug, but she had to allow he deserved it. This was a great idea.

'That *does* seem to cover pretty much everywhere. What time is it?'

'Just after one.'

'And they are one-day passes?'

'Yep.'

'Then we have no time to waste.' She whirled around to look at a nearby sign with a city map displayed on it. 'Okay. We need to approach this strategically. What is the nearest attraction?'

Akil stared at her, clearly bemused. 'You want to do it *all*?'

'Well,' she conceded. 'Maybe not *both* the theatre and the opera house, and obviously trying all the restaurants and all five of the walking tours would be a stretch, but let's try and do as much as we can before midnight when the tickets run out.'

'Is this a challenge?'

'Are you up to it?' She removed her sunglasses and met that cool amused gaze, her mouth responding automatically to the smile in his eyes.

'I'm an Ortiz. I never turn down a challenge.'

'Good to know. Okay, where shall we start? Where's nearest?'

'The castle.' He paused. 'Are you comfortable with that? Your father doesn't make a habit of crossing over into the public areas, but you never know. This might be the day he makes an exception. It could be awkward if you bumped into him in public.'

Clem bit her lip as she considered it. The castle was a much rebuilt and redesigned fortress perched on the edge of the valley overlooking the mountain pass that had once been the only way into the city. Most of it was now open to the public, who could tour the old staterooms, the rooms occupied by long-dead royalty, the courtyards and gardens, as well as the dungeons and defensive walls showcasing the country's often violent history.

But well away from the public areas were the royal apartments and the offices of the court, with a private entrance to parliament, whose equally impressive medieval building was right next door.

The royal apartments comprised living quarters for the King and his family as well as rooms for courtiers and staff and reception rooms for ambassadors and other dignitaries, plus rooms of varying sizes for official events.

As it was the parliamentary recess most parliamentarians and the aristocrats who made up the upper chamber were at home in their country estates or their seaside retreats. But the King, as Clem knew too well, rarely returned to the Palais d'Artega, staying at Court year-round. Which meant he might well be in the castle right now and she would be in the same building as him for the first time in almost a decade. But as a tourist she'd be as removed from him as she was when she was at home in Cornwall.

'He knows I'm here,' she said, trying to keep the bitterness from her voice. 'But to be honest he hasn't seen me for so long he'd be more likely to recognise you than me. Let's do it. I've always wanted to visit.'

She shook the lingering sadness off and consulted the map in front of them, tracing the routes with her finger. 'Okay, I propose we spend an hour in the castle, half an hour each in the cathedral and the city museum, get the cable car up the mountain and the funicular down and then take the railway to the zoo for the hour before closing time. If we leave promptly we should make the evening walking tour, which possibly gives us time for tonight's concert at the opera house. We'll need refreshments so a snack after we've gone up the cable car and dinner after the concert. What do you think?'

Akil pretended to sag against the post,

holding the map. 'I'm exhausted just listening to all that.'

'Too much for you?' She turned to face him, hands on her hips, allowing a flirtatious challenge to enter her voice, even as she acknowledged to herself that she was skating on very thin ice. This wasn't a date. But that didn't mean she couldn't enjoy it.

He held her gaze, suddenly serious, and Clem felt the air suck out of her lungs.

'Too much for me? Not at all. But I'm worried about you, my lady. Can you handle it?'

'It's my suggestion, remember. Come on, we're wasting precious time.' Clem rammed her sunglasses back onto her face, glad to break the disturbingly intense connection, and marched away, knowing he was right behind her, laughing as she strode as fast as she could as he effortlessly matched her stride. It was companionable. Nice.

She just needed to dial the flirting down to zero.

The castle was as fascinating and informative as Clem had hoped, and far more macabre than she'd expected, especially the dank underground rooms full of terrifying-looking devices.

'Nice types, my ancestors,' she muttered

as she took in the rusted manacles stained with what she fervently hoped wasn't blood.

Akil nodded. 'Mine too. Before they dominated parliament they were generals and military leaders. I bet they condemned a lot of people to these rooms.'

'What does that do?' She wandered over to a tall, beamed contraption hung with ropes to read the horribly visual interpretation board and shuddered. 'I could have quite happily lived without ever knowing that.'

'What kind of mind even invents something like that?' Akil was standing right behind her. At least two inches separated them, but she was acutely aware of every part of him, the proximity between them lighting up every nerve.

'No wonder they put this bit before the Crown jewels. We'll need all the glitter and pomp to wipe this out of our minds. If I never come down here again it's too soon.'

The tour led them through a bewildering array of corridors and courtyards and Akil kept her entertained with what Clem was pretty sure were completely made-up facts about every part. She couldn't remember the last time she'd laughed, really laughed, the last time it had been this easy to be with someone.

The last time it had been this easy to just be.

Finally they reached a dark, heavily guarded building where they followed the path around display cases filled with fur-trimmed cloaks and padded surcoats, jew-elled scabbards and wicked-looking swords until they reached a big display case set into a thick wall. Sightseers were kept well back by a rope, and, more effectively, guards at either end holding serious-looking rifles, in case anyone decided to try and steal the valuable items.

Clem stared at the state jewels in a mix-ture of awe and a painful melancholy, a sense of loss she couldn't quite explain. This was her family history but she had to see it as a paying tourist, always on the outside, held back by ropes and shatterproof glass and guards. She tried to hide her feelings, her voice unnaturally bright. 'The crown is huge! It must be really heavy. Like wearing a concrete hat.'

'It's very bling,' he said, blinking. 'I've seen it plenty of times but I'd never really noticed how many jewels it has before. And just how *gold* it is.'

'Maybe because the chain of office is equally bling.' Clem stared at the heavy gold chain studded with rubies. 'The sceptre is pretty big too. The whole lot together is very dazzling. I wouldn't say it's particularly tasteful though. All that velvet and gold and those huge rubies. It's a bit try hard.'

'The King makes it look so effortless,' Akil said. 'He makes the crown look like it weighs nothing. Whether you agree with him or not politically, he is good at what he does. He works well with the Assembly and controls the Senate. It needs a strong person to wear that crown.'

'Rosy is strong, one of the strongest people I know,' Clem said, still transfixed by the crown. 'But no one should have to bear that weight alone. If only I could be by her side, support her the way a sister should, make sure she wasn't alone. Seeing this makes it all much more understandable.'

'It all?'

'What she asked you. I almost wish…' She paused and he looked down at her, his expression inscrutable.

'What do you almost wish?'

'That things were different and you could have said yes…been what, who she needed.'

His expression didn't change, his eyes dark pools she was losing herself in. 'I could never have been who or what she needed. I knew it straight away, I think. I just had to work through it. And I am glad I realised in time.'

'In time?'

Clem couldn't breathe, couldn't move, all she could do was look up at him, so close she could see his dilated pupils, the rise and fall of his chest. It would be so easy to close the small distance between them and press herself against him but she was paralysed by the blood surging through her, the roaring in her ears.

'It's one thing to marry out of respect and friendship and support. They can be good bedrocks of a successful union, I believe that. But it would be unfair to marry one woman while attracted to her sister. Don't you think?'

Thinking was beyond her. She was caught in his mesmerising gaze, dark and hot, stirring desire throughout her. 'I…' She stared at him a moment longer, trying to find something to say—*I think you're attractive too.*

What does this mean? Kiss me—when the sound of a family approaching, children arguing noisily, broke the spell and Akil stepped back, a rueful smile on his lips.

'Come on,' he said. 'We've got a long itinerary and I think we're at least five minutes behind.'

Yet as they walked away she couldn't help but look back at the case and the glittering crown that represented her sister's future. Akil might find her attractive—and she might reciprocate his feelings—but she had no place, no future here. She couldn't let herself forget it.

CHAPTER SEVEN

AKIL COULDN'T REMEMBER the last time he'd enjoyed an afternoon so much nor the last time he'd had the leisure—or inclination—to dedicate a day to nothing but fun. It had been a genius plan to explore his city with fresh eyes, joining the tourists on the well-trodden trails around the sights. They'd done a mad dash around the cathedral and the city museum and made up the lost time as they did so because—as Clem said a little guiltily—there were only so many religious paintings a person could admire before they all merged into one.

'Do you think they'd ever actually seen a baby before?' she asked as they checked out their twentieth old master rendition of a Madonna and Child, this one with a baby Jesus almost the same size as his mother. The one before the baby had been the approximate size of an orange. 'They remind me of my attempts of art at school and I always got a *Could do better*. Who knew I was actually painting in the style of the fourteenth century? My teachers should have given me more credit.'

After the museum they enjoyed the breathtaking views from the cable car that ascended up to the mountain shelf overlooking the city, a popular day-trip destination, where they stopped for a snack before taking the funicular back down and catching the small steam train to the zoo.

'I have very conflicted feelings about zoos,' Clem said as they wandered around the world-renowned attraction, known for its ground-breaking breeding programmes and successful conservation work. 'I know that if this tiger wasn't here it wouldn't be roaming free in the jungle, it wouldn't exist at all. And I know that if it wasn't for places like this there might be no tigers at all in a few years' time, but it seems wrong to see such beautiful creatures caged up, for us to be able to stand and stare while they have nowhere to hide.'

Her face softened as she watched the tiger

prowl, its tail swishing irritably. 'I wish I could set you free.'

'Now that would make an interesting headline. *Fake Princess Sets Tiger on Horrified Population.*' He gave her a keen glance. 'Do you think you might be over identifying?'

'Hmm?'

'Beautiful creature locked away?'

She laughed a little nervously. 'I'm not...'

'Beautiful? I hope you know that's not true.'

Their glances caught and held and Akil could feel his blood thundering around his body as her cheeks pinked, her pupils dilated. He'd felt in his very bones that this attraction was not one-sided, but her reaction gave him all the proof he needed. Primal jubilation filled him as he ran one finger slowly down her cheek. She stood acquiescent, quivering under his touch, her gaze still fixed on his.

'Akil...' Her voice was husky, half protest half entreaty, and he dropped his hand, fighting the urge to pull her close, to taste those full lips. 'I...' She cleared her throat, adorably flustered, still flushed a rosy pink. 'I was going to say locked away. I can get out, you know, it's just not easy. Besides, it's only temporary. Come on, we need to get on or we'll miss the walking tour.'

'Yes, ma'am.' He saluted. 'Begging your pardon for forgetting the itinerary, ma'am.'

She threw him a mock stern look. 'I'll let you off this once.'

Despite Clem's protestation that they would be late, Akil insisted on stopping at the food cart at the zoo exit to buy them tart chilled lemonade and toasted cheese sandwiches, hot and oozing with melted cheese.

'We've walked miles already and your schedule doesn't allow for dinner until after the opera,' he said as he handed her the sandwich. 'A man's got to eat. Especially this man.'

'That's good to know about you. Hangry unless fed, noted. Mmm, that's delicious.' She took another, bigger bite, laughing as she tried not to spill any cheese on her dress, and Akil couldn't help but join in as he watched her inelegantly scoop up a glop of cheese with her tongue.

It had been a long time since he'd laughed this much, talked this much, about nothing and everything. Clem was easy company— apart from the way his body reacted to her every move, the way he wanted to pull her close and kiss her until they were both breathless.

But she was here for such a short while and her life was complicated enough. It wasn't for him to complicate it further than he already had and it would be too easy to do so, considering how thrown she'd been when he'd told her how attractive he found her.

'You are very good at saluting,' Clem said as they walked along the pretty pedestrianised street that led back to the centre, flowers in planters on either side and leafy trees protecting them from the worst of the sun.

'You can thank national service for that.'

'Of course. It seems so strange to me that you have to give up two years of your life! Even Rosy had to enlist before she went to university.'

'Every Asturian does, even royalty. Your sister and mine worked in the medical corps together. But it wasn't two years for me, it was four. Two in the infantry, like all good Ortiz men, then two in the secret service. I came out at twenty-two to go to university.'

'What did you study?'

'Economics and politics of course.'

'Of course. Was that what you wanted to do?'

And that was the million-dollar question. Usually Akil went along with the fiction that studying politics in readiness for taking the Ortiz seat in the upper house was his own ambition. It was easier that way.

But he didn't want to dissimulate with Clem. It was nice having someone he could be himself with. 'Truthfully no. I had a place at medical school.'

'Really? Like your sister?'

'Only I'm older and got my place first, so really she was copying me.' He couldn't help grinning as he said it. 'The sibling rivalry between us is real. Elixane hates that she's both four years younger than me and a girl in a country which still favours male heirs.'

'You should be flattered that she wanted to follow in your footsteps. It's nice that you inspire her.'

'I don't think she'd put it that way, but I'll be sure to mention it to her.' His grin widened as he imagined his sister's indignant response if he referred to himself as her inspiration. 'Honestly, I'm not sure why we both chose that path. There are no medics in the family.'

'So what happened? Why didn't you take up your place?'

Akil carried on walking, deliberating how much to say. He rarely allowed himself to think about that time. 'I don't know if you know this, but the seats in the Senate, our upper chamber, are hereditary—and the line of inheritance is on the male side. Even when things change next month those seats which belong to the old aristocratic titles, like mine, will only go to males—it's the same in the UK.'

'I am beginning to sympathise with your sister,' Clem murmured.

'We're making some headway in reforming this, but we have a long way to go.'

'Of course,' she said consideringly. 'Inheritance really should go through the matriarchal line. Before DNA testing, it was obvious who the mother was but the father was taken on trust.'

'You would get on far too well with my sister, she often makes the same point, although, as I tell her, I am still older and that makes me the head of the family and future Duc no matter if the law changed.'

'I'll bet she loves that.'

'She really does, although occasionally

she will admit that she is much happier as a younger sibling—there's a lot more freedom for her than for me. But what you need to understand is that the Duc d'Ortiz has always been an important person in Asturia, for centuries we were in charge of the military. Sometimes the Duc was the Crown's right hand, even Regent on two occasions, sometimes its most implacable opposition. Since the Second World War, as Asturia's military need has waned, my family have turned to politics to build power and influence, with the Duc using his hereditary seat to make sure they are right at the centre. My father made it clear that I was shirking the responsibility inherent in my future title by not pursuing politics.'

Clem frowned. 'But your father is still alive, right? So why couldn't you do both? Be a doctor now and then a politician later?'

Exactly what he had pointed out eight years ago. 'My father is not a man to do things by half, not work, not food, not drink.' Not women. 'Nor is he a man to take his doctor's advice. He has little time for the medical profession. He sees it as a job for the bourgeoisie, not his heir. His health was not good eight years ago so when we disagreed and it got far too heated he collapsed. He nearly died of a heart attack.'

A heart attack Akil had known was a risk, and yet he still hadn't walked away when the argument had started to get out of hand, had still allowed all his anger at his father, at his selfishness and implacability, to pour out. Had enjoyed reducing his father to incoherent rage, out-arguing him. What kind of man did that make him? No better than his father for all his self-righteousness.

Clem stopped, her hand flying to her mouth as she turned to him. 'Oh, Akil, I am so sorry. It must have been terrifying.'

'It was. Worse was the knowledge that I was responsible.'

Her forehead creased. 'How? You said yourself that he didn't take his doctor's advice. Surely that's on him.'

'True,' he acknowledged. 'But I was young and implacable as only the young can be, convinced I alone knew the right path. I wanted to be a doctor and yet I allowed a man I knew to be at risk to get agitated to lose control. Worse, I goaded him. Pushed him beyond what was safe. What kind of son, what kind of aspiring doctor, does that?'

'Families make everything complicated.

We're not always our best selves with them,' she said, laying a comforting hand on his arm. 'So you gave up your dream? As what? Atonement?'

In part. 'I promised him that if he just held on I would do my duty as the Vicomte d'Ortiz. So when he recovered he stepped down on grounds of ill health and the Senate voted to allow me to take the Ortiz seat early. My father now spends most of his time in Switzerland still not looking after his health and I am as you see me. Fulfilling my promise.'

'Do you ever regret it?'

'I don't allow myself to regret it.' Suddenly he regretted saying so much. 'Come, there's still a lot to fit in.' Without looking back, he marched on. Because that was what he did, eyes fixed on the future, no dwelling on the past. It was easier that way. It was safer. It was what he knew.

Clem stole a glance at Akil as they walked towards the medieval square where the walking tour was due to meet. He'd been silent over the last few minutes, seemingly lost in thought.

Not that it was surprising. It must be hard,

living one life when you had once had a vocation for something else. But then again wasn't that the future she was facing? It would be some consolation if she was as successful in her second-choice career as Akil was in his.

But she still ached with sympathy for him. Maybe it was better having a father as hands off as hers rather than one who raged and manipulated and used a promise extracted on a possible deathbed to push his son down a path he didn't want. And it wasn't as if Akil wanted to give it all up to become a pop star or something equally ridiculous! He wanted to be a doctor—every parent she knew would throw a party if their child expressed such a wish.

Her mother would have. She'd supported Clem, it hadn't been in her nature not to, but she'd have preferred Clem to have chosen something more worthy than acting.

She peeked at Akil again; his expression was still far away. 'What's the tour?' she asked, wanting to break the silence.

He blinked as if he had forgotten where they were going. 'Hmm? Oh, the twilight tour. Apparently it's ghosts, ghouls and gore. Ready?'

She pulled a face. 'I'm not sure I can face ghouls and gore after the dungeons earlier. I'm already dreading the nightmares.'

'This is our heritage. We should embrace it.'

'Not too enthusiastically, I hope.'

'We don't have to go on the tour,' he reminded her. 'We could always skip it and do something else.'

'Skip it? And lose the challenge? Absolutely not.'

'Of course.' She was relieved to hear laughter in his voice. 'The schedule. How could I forget?'

'So this finishes at seven, conveniently right by the opera house, which gives us time to get our tickets. I hope they're not sold out. What is it?'

Akil pulled out his phone and checked. 'There are tickets and it's *Tosca*—oh, good, there's a warning. Contains depictions of torture, murder and suicide. There's a definite theme to the day so far.'

'In that case I want to eat at the cheesiest, most kitsch restaurant as possible afterwards,' Clem warned him. 'I'll need it after all the horror and death.'

'I'll see what I can do,' he promised.

They lapsed into another silence, but this one was more companionable, their stride perfectly in time, arms swinging together, so close their fingers almost touched. Almost.

As they entered the square she saw a small group of people waiting by the meeting point. A couple of families, several older couples and a young couple who smiled as Akil and Clem approached. They probably saw a mirror of themselves, a couple enjoying a romantic break in the picturesque ancient city, and Clem allowed herself to bask in the fantasy that she and Akil were here properly together. Before she thought better of it she reached out and took his hand, slipping her fingers through his. She felt him momentarily freeze before his fingers clasped hers, warm and strong, his thumb circling the back of her hand, a minute gesture that shuddered through her.

'Okay, gather round.' A tour guide dressed in the colourful Asturian national costume called out in English and then again in French. 'Does everyone have their tickets ready? Great. Okay, let's begin right here, with the great siege of 1412.'

Despite the theme the tour was a lot of fun, the guide engaging as well as knowledgeable, and Clem found herself laughing uncontrollably as he took them on a whistle-stop tour of the least palatable parts of Asturian history, pitching his spiel perfectly between scaring the children just enough and amusing the adults. Throughout the tour she was aware of Akil's hand in hers, the breadth of him, height of him, the sheer handsomeness of him taking her breath away, the wonder that he wanted to be here with her—the wonder that he wanted her—dizzying her. Possibility hung thick between them, the possibility that this adventure wouldn't end when the tickets expired at midnight, but this Cinderella might keep her bewitched existence a little longer.

Just a few hours ago she had been reminding herself that she had no future here, warning herself to be careful, but now those sensible thoughts belonged to someone else. What did the future matter when there was now?

The group clustered around a cannon that pointed out towards the mountain pass and was, they were informed, haunted by a young soldier who had refused to abandon his post when the city was under attack and stayed there still to protect Asturia.

The guide's voice had dropped to a carrying whisper as he told the tale and the children on the tour pressed forward, eyes wide in the deepening dusk, only to jump back in exaggerated fright when he boomed out the end. As they jumped, one tripped and before anyone could catch her fell into the road—and straight into the path of a car. Time seemed to slow as the small body was scooped up onto the low bonnet as the car screeched to a desperate but too late halt.

Everyone was paralysed with shock and fear—everyone but Akil. He dropped Clem's hand and sprang into the road even as the car finally braked, shouting instructions to call an ambulance. He bent over the girl, his finger on her neck, and then ran his hands carefully over her.

'Stay back, she needs space,' he called out. 'Where are her parents?' An American couple were at his side in seconds, one holding a smaller girl, faces pale and shocked. 'She's breathing,' he reassured them. 'That's a good thing. Her leg is certainly broken, and I can't rule out internal bleeding or concussion, but the hospital isn't far.'

'Are you a doctor?' the woman asked, and

Clem was proud to see he didn't wince as he shook his head.

'No, but I volunteer with the mountain rescue and I am paramedic trained. She'll be in good hands, I promise.'

It took the ambulance less than ten minutes to arrive and Clem stayed back as Akil assisted the paramedics as they moved the still unconscious girl onto the trolley and checked her over. The rest of the group were still huddled together, silent, and as she was loaded into the ambulance Akil came over.

'I am going to accompany her to the hospital,' he told Clem quietly. 'Her parents don't speak Asturian or French and it will be helpful for them to have a translator.'

'Of course,' she said hurriedly. 'I told Henri I'd call him as soon as we were done, so he can collect me and I can transform back on the way back to the palais. It's dark now so I only need to get through the gates and the guards never check Henri anyway.'

'I'm sorry we didn't make the opera.'

'Another time.' But even as she said it she could feel the possibility slipping away. In the cold light of day would this live-for-the-moment promise she had made to herself last? Or would she remember all the reasons getting close to Akil—to anyone in Asturia—was such a bad idea?

Akil drew her close, his arm an anchor. 'Of course. We'll rearrange and we can pick up our schedule. Carry on as we planned.'

'That would be lovely.' She could hear the lack of conviction in her words and she knew he heard it too. Before she could back away he bent his head and brushed her mouth with his. It was the briefest of caresses, almost chaste, but the touch lit her up, flames swooshing through her from the tips of her fingers to the ends of her toes. All she could do was look up dazed as Akil smiled ruefully and stepped away. 'I'll see you soon.'

Clem stared after him, drinking in his tall figure, allowing herself one last look at the way his jeans encased him so perfectly, the fit of his T-shirt, the strength and grace in the fully muscled body. She swallowed, fighting the need to run after him, to call his name, to kiss him once again. Instead she watched him step into the ambulance and exchange a few words with the paramedic before the doors shut and he was driven away.

'Goodbye,' she said at last. But whether she meant for tonight or for keeps, she didn't know.

CHAPTER EIGHT

IT WAS LATE by the time Clem returned to the villa but despite her exhaustion she found it hard to sleep, replaying the events of the day over and over, lingering on the brief kiss until she had no idea what was memory and what was fantasy. When she finally got up the next day she was convinced she hadn't slept at all, and her activity watch confirmed her suspicions. With a groan she took her coffee and a book onto the comfortable terrace sofa and curled up, promising herself a lazy day.

She'd messaged Akil last night to check on the injured girl and he'd promised to send her an update. To her relief when she checked her phone, she found a message from Akil sent some time early that morning letting her know that although the girl's leg was broken and she'd severely bruised her ribs, there was no internal bleeding and she'd somehow managed to avoid concussion. The hospital were going to keep her in for several days for observation but she'd been very lucky.

Clem pressed the reply arrow and then sat there for some time staring at the blank screen before typing a simple thank-you. After another couple of minutes' thought she added:

You were brilliant yesterday.

Before she could think better of it she sent the message and then lay back on the sofa and stared up at the cloudless sky, mind an exhausted whirl.

What would have happened if there had been no accident? Would they have gone to the opera? For dinner? Would possibility have hung in the air throughout? Would she have gone back to Akil's apartment? And if so, then what?

She'd never know...

At that moment her phone vibrated and when she picked it up her sister's name filled the screen. Clem took a deep breath and then answered it, injecting as much vibrancy into her voice as she possibly could.

'Hi, you, what are you up to?'

'Just checking in,' her sister said, and Clem felt some of the tension leave her as she took in just how relaxed Arrosa sounded. 'Is everything okay with you? Have you heard from our father yet?'

'Not yet.' Clem tried to sound breezy, as if the continued silence didn't bother her at all, but of course her sister knew better and she didn't try and hide her sigh of exasperation.

'Honestly, what's he playing at? Do you want me to say something?'

'No, no, it's fine.' Clem *did* want to see him, but more, she wanted *him* to want to see *her*, not for him to pay her a duty visit because his other, legitimate daughter had scolded him into doing it. 'There's plenty of time yet. I'm sure we'll catch up sooner rather than later.'

'You're sure? And you're fine to stay? It's been a week now and I feel a lot better so if you're bored of being driven around like a ceremonial doll, just say.'

'I'm fine. It's very relaxing sitting in the back of a limousine in designer clothing, so let me enjoy it a little longer. What have you been up to anyway? Did you and Sally have that cinema trip? And did the theatre action group find somewhere else to meet?'

Clem sat back and sipped her coffee as Arrosa filled her in on all the local news and told her all about meeting Sally for a couple of drinks at the local pub. Not exactly the most rock and roll evening for a single twenty-six-year-old, but probably the most freedom her sister had had in years.

'Clem?' A diffident note had entered her sister's voice and Clem put her coffee down, all senses on alert. 'What do you know about Jack Treloar?'

'Jack Treloar? As in our "local bad boy done good, trying to take over the town theatre and commercialise it" Jack Treloar?'

'That's the one.'

Clem's first instinct was to demand an explanation why Arrosa was interested in *Jack Treloar* of all people but, knowing what it must have cost Rosy to ask the question and provoke the inevitable reaction, she made herself hold back.

'Not much,' she said, sifting through her scant knowledge and trying to exclude gossip and hearsay. 'He's about four years older than me so we were never in the same school year and didn't hang around with the same group, although from what I remember he was always quite solitary. His dad was absent a lot, drifted in and out of his life, his mother did her best but he had a real reputation. If there was ever any trouble it was attributed to him. Then he took up with the local bigwig's daughter, next thing she was pregnant and they got married. I don't think they were more than eighteen, it was quite the scandal. They disappeared off to London where somehow he made money hand over fist. I think she died tragically a couple of years back, then six months ago he returned with his daughters and bought the most expensive house in the village. No one knows why he came back. Goodness knows he can't have many happy memories of living in Cornwall. He left the town under the shadow of a scandal and has returned the same, especially now he's trying to strong-arm the council into selling or leasing the theatre to him.'

She paused before giving in and asking the burning question. 'Why? How have you come across him? He usually doesn't descend from his clifftop mansion to mix with us mere mortals.'

'He was at your play, so sometimes he does. Anyway, I've found myself babysitting for his daughters,' Arrosa said, an evasive tone in her voice, and Clem nearly choked on her coffee.

'You are *what*? How on earth did that come about?'

'It's a long story. I'll fill you in some other time.'

'I've got time now,' Clem offered, but her sister was clearly not going to be drawn.

'Honestly, it's not very interesting. But what *is* interesting is what's going on with you. Has the gorgeous Akil contacted you yet?'

'I didn't think that you thought he was that good-looking,' Clem countered, and her sister laughed.

'Objectively I can see that he is, but more importantly I know that you think so. Come on, spill the beans, what's going on? He asked for your number a couple of days ago. Has he been in contact?'

'We met up yesterday but nothing is going on, he's just being kind.' It was Clem's turn to prevaricate as her sister let out a disbelieving— and most un-princess-like—snort.

'If you say so. I've known Akil a long

time and he has a real sense of honour and justice, but I wouldn't have called him kind, not in the "give up a second afternoon to entertain a stranger" way.'

'I don't know, it seems completely in character to me. Did you know that he works for the mountain rescue?'

'I've seen it mentioned in interviews, but he's usually pretty quiet about it. Not really one for sharing at all. So he's mentioned it to you, has he?'

'I saw him in action. There was an accident and I just froze, it was horrid, but he knew exactly what to do. It was impressive.'

'Handsome and heroic. He's quite the catch.'

'Rosy. Tell me honestly, are you having second thoughts?'

Clem held her breath while she waited for her sister's answer. Arrosa and Akil belonged in the same world, the same social circles, the higher echelons of the same country, had shared goals. It would make perfect sense for her sister to have reconsidered, and if she did then it would be Clem's duty to step aside and hide her own feelings. She might not be a princess, but she was a princess's sister and she knew what that entailed. She'd seen the weight of that crown yesterday.

'Not a second or a third or a fourth thought,' Arrosa said emphatically. 'And I can tell you something, nor is he.'

'How do you know?' Clem hoped her sister couldn't hear how desperately she wanted that to be true.

'Because he's attracted to *you*, Clem. It was so obvious when I spoke to him. And it's obvious that you like him so what kind of sister would I be if I came between you, even if that's what I wanted? Which for the record I don't.'

'He kissed me,' Clem confessed and winced as her sister let out a whoop.

'I knew it!'

'It was only a brief kiss goodbye as he was heading for the ambulance.'

'But you wanted more?'

Clem closed her eyes and relived the feeling of his mouth brushing hers again. 'Yes,' she confessed.

'This is *marvellous*. I'm so excited for you. What's the next step? When are you going to see him again?'

'I don't know, Rosy.' Clem tried to gather her racing thoughts. 'Akil lives such a dif-

ferent life from me. For a start he lives in a
different country. And he knows what he
wants while I'm floundering. He has his
life all planned out. Plus, he wants a well-
connected wife who knows his world and
understands politics and diplomacy. I'm a
walking national scandal. That's the last
thing he needs.'

'I hate that you see yourself that way,' Arrosa said softly.

'It's not how I see myself, it's how others
see me. It's how our father sees me, how the
very few people in the court who know I
even exist see me. The truth is that although
Akil can squire me around he couldn't be
seen with me anywhere that matters. We
both know that's true. So what future could
we possibly have?'

There was a startled pause. 'You feel that
strongly about him? Are you falling in love
with him, Clem?'

'Am I *what*?' Clem winced as she realised
just how ridiculous she was being. 'I've only
met him twice, of course I'm not. In lust,
yes, and I like him a lot. But it's way too
early to even think about love.'

'In that case,' Arrosa said, 'what's the

harm in spending some time with him? What's the worst that could happen, Clem?'

He might reject me because of who I am. He might realise I'm not good enough.

But of course she couldn't say that aloud, not even to the sister she loved.

'You're right,' she said instead. 'I'm being a drama queen. It comes with the job, you know that. But if I see Akil again will you promise me something? Be careful with Jack Treloar.'

'Only if you promise *not* to be careful.' And, laughing, her sister hung up, leaving Clem staring at her phone. She hadn't lied to Rosy; it *was* far too early to think about love. But she was in far deeper than two meetings should warrant and that left heartbreak as an inevitable outcome.

She would allow herself to see what, if anything, happened next, but she would guard her heart and her soul. It was the only way to keep herself safe.

It had been another long night. By the time Lucy, the injured American girl, had been settled in and checked, and all her family's questions answered and concerns addressed, it had been after three a.m. Akil had stumbled back to his apartment, luckily less than half a mile away, and collapsed on the sofa, where he'd fallen into a deep sleep only to awaken three hours later when Tiger had jumped on him and insistently demanded some breakfast. Akil had drunk some water and eaten the very last of the bread before sending the promised text to Clem to fill her in on Lucy's progress, and falling back asleep. He'd woken a couple of hours later, neck stiff but feeling refreshed. Coffee, a quick shower and change of clothes and he was ready for the day ahead.

But for once, for the first time in longer than he could remember, he had no plans. There was of course work, recess or no recess his inbox was overflowing, but his assistants were filtering it for him and there was nothing urgent to address. He wasn't rostered in to be on call with the mountain rescue and wouldn't be again until next week after all the shifts he'd recently pulled.

He strode around the apartment restlessly, his gaze falling on the poetry book Clem had looked at just the day before, and smiled wryly. Maybe he'd unconsciously kept the time free in case he and Clem wanted to spend another day together. After all, if things had gone the way they'd been heading last night, she might have been here with him now. They might have been planning another day of exploring and getting to know each other. Or they might still have been in bed.

It was an intoxicating thought. He wasn't sure why the Englishwoman had got under his skin like this. She was beautiful, yes, but he knew plenty of beautiful women. It went beyond a physical attraction. She was both funny and straight talking, a combination he appreciated, and there was a hidden vulnerability that made him want to take care of her, to make her smile, to make her feel appreciated.

Goodness knew, someone should. It might be none of his business but one day Akil would tell Zorien exactly what he thought of his parenting style.

He picked up his phone and reread the message she'd sent in reply to his update.

Are you free? If so come over. Let's go out.

He should reply, but he just wasn't sure what to say. Or was it actually better that last night had been cut short? Was it safer for them both not to take this attraction between them further? There was no future after all.

But did he always need to plan for the long term? Couldn't he occasionally just enjoy life as it was. It was summer; she was here for a finite time. Why was he overcomplicating this?

One thing he did know: he wasn't going to make any sensible decisions on an empty stomach.

Akil headed out of the apartment, popping into one of the many local cafes for a quick savoury pastry and a small cup of the potent espresso Asturians loved. It took him less than a minute to finish his breakfast and he decided to go back to the hospital and check in on Lucy and her family before making any further plans. Clem would want to know how they were, after all.

Lucy had been placed in a small private room, and Akil made his way there, stopping to chat with a couple of the nurses and a doctor he knew and catching up with one of his fellow volunteers who had just finished a shift. It was nearly lunch time by the time he reached the children's ward to be buzzed in by a nurse who recognised him. Lucy's door was ajar and to his surprise he could hear a familiar voice within. What was Clem doing here?

He stood there for a moment, pleasure and apprehension warring inside him. Whatever happened next between them would be decided soon whether he was ready or not. As he waited, he began to make sense of the words within and he realised that Clem was reading to the small girl. He stepped a little closer and leaned against the door frame listening.

She was good, very good, her rich voice bringing the text to life, giving each character a distinct voice. Lucy was still pale, her leg extended before her, lines of pain on her small face, but she was smiling, looking eagerly at Clem as Clem continued to read, clearly transported to the magical world Clem was bringing vividly to life. Akil waited until the end of the chapter before pushing the door further open and entering the room, not wanting to break the spell Clem cast.

'How's the patient?' he asked in English and Lucy smiled at him.

'Clem came to read to me. She's really good.'

Clem met his eye although her expression

was adorably flustered and she'd reddened. 'I wanted to see how Lucy was doing so got Henri to drop me near here. I didn't expect to be allowed in but I saw her mother outside getting some air. Her family seemed exhausted so I insisted that they went back to the hotel to get some food and a change of clothes and promised I'd keep an eye on her.'

Akil eyed the small girl keenly. 'She seems to be doing pretty well, but she looks like she needs a bit of a rest. Do you want to try to get some sleep, Lucy? We will wait just outside until your parents get back so if you need anything or you get lonely just press that button.'

'I am a little sleepy,' the little girl admitted. 'But can we read another chapter later, Clem?'

'Of course.' Clem brushed her fringe back and smiled down at the wan face. 'I'd love to. Are you comfy? Those pillows okay?' Akil watched as she expertly settled the child with soothing hands. Of course, she'd helped care for her mother and recently too. Being here must bring back some difficult memories. His admiration for her deepened.

Once Lucy was settled, Akil steered Clem out to the comfortable chairs in the adjacent waiting room. 'You want a coffee or anything?'

'No, I'm fine. How about you? What time did you get to bed?'

Akil grimaced. 'Not so much bed, more the sofa, but I've had some sleep. It was kind of you to come and check on Lucy. Even kinder to offer to watch her.'

Clem brushed the compliment aside. 'Not at all. I've spent a lot of time waiting in hospitals, I know how time takes a different element here. And her parents have another child who was definitely at the exhausted and fractious stage. I wasn't sure how they'd feel about leaving Lucy with me, but I managed to persuade them that they would be much more use to her if they were rested, fed and changed. I don't think her mother will be gone long, but a shower and time away from here will do her good.'

'It was a clever idea to read to her. You definitely put her at her ease.'

'It was no big deal. I actually really enjoyed doing it.' She sounded surprised and he quirked an eyebrow at her.

'You're an actress, don't you grab at any opportunity to perform?'

'After my mum died, I didn't think I'd

ever want to set foot in a hospital again. But now I'm here, I'm remembering all the things that helped. All the volunteers as well as the nurses who made such unbearable times surprisingly bearable. The value of having people who would sit with Maman just to listen, to be there, allowing her to say all the things she couldn't say to me. The same for me, people who would listen when I was angry or selfish or frustrated. That was invaluable, priceless. Reading to one small girl is a very, very small way of giving back.'

She looked so small, almost defenceless, and yet there was an indomitable spirit about her that he was drawn to. In two steps he was next to her, drawing her up into his arms. Akil looked down into the heart-shaped face, at the gold-flecked eyes shadowed with exhaustion, and knew that for once he didn't care what the future held, he wanted her, he needed her, and by some miracle she wanted him too.

'It wasn't small to Lucy or her family. It was everything.'

'Being here is helping me too. It might be a different hospital in a different country but the smell, the look, is pretty much universal. It's making me realise how my life pretty much just stopped eighteen months ago. No wonder I don't know what to do next, I've forgotten how to move forward. But I'm ready, Akil. I'm ready to live, not just exist at last.'

She cupped his face with her hands. They were warm against his skin, the gentle touch setting him on fire, and he closed his eyes briefly to allow the sensation to soak in.

'Help me live again, Akil,' she whispered, and he was helpless against her soft entreaty, against her touch.

Slowly, deliberately, not wanting to rush a single moment, he dipped his head and captured her full inviting mouth with his for a second time. But this was no mere brush, no promise, but an intent and she responded in kind, opening up to him, her hands moving to the nape of his neck as he moulded her body to his. He pulled back slightly to look down at her, eyes glazed, mouth parted.

'Anything,' he promised her. 'Whatever you want, whatever you need, anything.' And he kissed her again, the sounds of the hospital fading away, the feel of her, the taste of her all he wanted, all he knew.

CHAPTER NINE

CLEM TURNED IN to the pretty medieval square where Akil lived, aware of Henri standing watching her, making sure she was okay. It was funny how used to his discreet presence she'd got, no longer troubled by the knowledge that even when she couldn't see him he was only a few seconds away. The only time he wasn't close by was when she was with Akil. His secret service training meant that Henri usually didn't accompany them, although he was always on call and, she suspected, never that far away.

They'd fallen into a routine over the last couple of weeks. Every morning Henri drove her out, ostensibly to the court but in reality facilitating the discreet change that allowed her to explore the country with Akil or head to the hospital, often both, then reversing the process late each evening. Her life couldn't be more different from that first lonely week. Now her days were packed. She spent a lot of time at the hospital; Lucy had been discharged over a week ago to fly home, but news of Clem's reading had spread throughout the children's ward and she now did a group session for those in the big general ward. She enjoyed it far more than she had expected to. It wasn't acting exactly, but she was transporting them into other worlds, creating magic, and that, for Clem, was as fulfilling as a big production, although if she had more time she would have liked to look into doing something bigger, maybe trying to stage some kind of small production. The volunteering was certainly opening up some possibilities and, although she was deliberately not worrying about the future just yet, ideas were percolating away.

And when she wasn't at the hospital she was with Akil. He still volunteered two days a week, and spent most mornings buried in his inbox, but the afternoons and evenings were hers. They had finally made it to the opera and to the theatre—this time a comedy, much to her relief—and to several friendly neighbourhood restaurants, the kind where a prominent politician wouldn't expect to be photographed. Any high-profile venues were out, any events where society people mingled too dangerous, but Akil was sure that if they stuck to the tourist trail no one would give them a second glance. So far that had been true, and it was getting easier and easier to forget that she was here under false pretences and not a tourist at all.

They'd hiked some of the mountain trails, pausing for cold beers and well-stuffed sandwiches at the cafes at the summit, and explored some of the picture-perfect villages and towns dotted throughout valleys and mountain shelves, cliff tops and riversides. One day they kayaked along a river, racing each other, another day they abseiled down a mountainside. She felt fitter and more resilient than she had for a long, long time.

And then there was Akil himself, his slow smile and intent gaze, his sure touch and sweet, sweet kisses. They were still at the courting phase, and although their kisses and caresses were getting increasingly heated— and increasingly intimate—neither had been in any rush to move to the next stage. It was as if they had all the time in the world.

Only of course they didn't.

Checking her watch, Clem realised she

was a little early so rather than head straight to Akil's apartment she decided to have a little explore around the neighbourhood. He lived in a charming part of the old quarter, filled with cafes and local artisan shops. Just the kind of place she liked.

Fixing her sunglasses firmly on her nose, Clem headed along the nearest alley, emerging into a narrow cobbled street. Cafes and shops nestled next to each other, the old buildings four storeys high, their upper levels lurching drunkenly over the street. This part of the city was centuries old, the country's history in every cobble, every plastered and timbered front, the butchers and tanners giving way to tourist-friendly jewellers and art galleries. Clem moved slowly along, enjoying examining all the enticing wares laid out in the shop windows, the sun warming her arms, the sounds of the city a lively soundtrack.

She paused in front of a jeweller and examined the tree-inspired bracelets in silver and gold. Her mother would have loved them. Everything she'd worn had had some kind of link to nature whether it was the floral prints she'd preferred or the delicate swallow earring she'd always worn. Maybe she should buy one. Not that she needed jewellery to remember her mother, but she couldn't resist the impulse and headed in, emerging a few moments later clutching a bag, having bought a bracelet for herself and one for her sister, and a pair of cufflinks for Akil. They weren't really at the present stage, but she wanted him to have something to remember her by when this was all over.

Finally she stopped to look at some delicious pastries, her mouth watering at the sight of the nut and honey confections; she'd developed a taste for the local delicacies over the last couple of weeks. She couldn't resist popping in to buy some and they were still warm when she returned to the square and rang the buzzer to Akil's apartment. She took the now familiar stairs up to his first-floor apartment two at a time and as she reached Akil's front door he opened it.

'Hi,' she said a little stupidly as he leaned against the door frame, his dark eyes glowing in admiration as he looked her up and down. Clem resisted the urge to smooth her shirt down, glad she'd picked the floaty sunshine-yellow silk skirt and teamed it with a short delicate lace white blouse. It wasn't the most practical of outfits, but she liked how feminine she felt, liked the way the skirt swirled around her calves, the flattering fit of the shirt, deceptively demure with its high neck, yet cut to flatter her every curve—and Akil's not too subtle once-over proved it did.

'Hi. You're looking beautiful today.' His voice was a low rumble and she felt it vibrate through her.

'Thank you. You're not looking too bad yourself.' Now that was an understatement. He was delectably handsome in a white linen shirt and jeans, off duty and perfectly masculine. 'I've bought pastries.' She handed him the bag and he unleashed one of his devastating smiles.

'Now you're doubly welcome.' He bent his head to drop a lingering kiss on her mouth and her body responded enthusiastically. This kind of passion was so different from anything she'd experienced she'd never actually gone weak at the knees before.

Clem entered the apartment and headed straight over to Tiger, who uttered a miaow as she reached him, stretching out so that she could reach his cream and ginger tummy.

'Hello, gorgeous,' she crooned, and Tiger stretched even further demanding worship. 'How are you?'

'Is it wrong I'm jealous of my cat?' Akil asked and she threw him a mischievous grin.

'Cats need to be paid their dues first, you know that.'

She continued to croon at Tiger while Akil put the pastries onto a plate and poured fresh coffee, bringing them over to her and sitting next to her on the big leather sofa. She loved the domesticity of it, cuddling up to him, ignoring the world outside.

'How was the hospital this morning?'

'Good. There's a couple of new kids in, but they came to the reading. I still can't believe that this is something I do! I keep waiting for someone to ask who I am and why I'm there. To throw me out.'

'They're always looking for ways to make it an easier experience for the children. And don't worry, I vouched for you.'

'And it's that easy? No background check, no references?'

'You're not alone with the children at any time, are you?'

'No, of course not. But I didn't mean for it to get to be a regular thing. What happens when I leave in three weeks' time?'

'I'm on the hospital board…'

She turned to face him. 'You never said.'

He shrugged. 'It didn't come up.' No wonder no one had challenged her presence. 'But you've shown that we have a need for this kind of entertainment, maybe in more than the children's ward. It's being looked at.'

'Look at me influencing hospital policy.'

'You have good instincts and a good heart. It would never have occurred to me if you hadn't shown me the way.'

An unexpected pride washed over her. She might not be the Crown Princess, but she might have achieved some good in the time she was in her sister's country.

'So what's the plan for today?' she asked as she finished the pastry.

Akil flashed a grin at her. 'I was thinking that it's time I introduced you to the most important woman in my life.'

Clem stiffened. His *what*? Surely he didn't mean his mother? She had never got the impression that they were that close and it was way too early—and too temporary—for that, and wasn't his sister abroad? He must have seen her alarm because he hastily added, 'My boat.'

That was more like it. 'I love boats. Did you know I grew up by the sea?'

'You may have mentioned it a hundred

times or more, which is why I hoped you would like this idea. Then it's a date?'

'Absolutely!'

'Let's pick up some provisions, then…'

'Look at you with the nautical terms.'

'I'll have no insubordination on my ship, thank you. Tell Henri I'll drive you back. It may be late.'

She saluted, her smile cheeky. 'Yes, Captain. Anything you say, Captain.' With a roar he pinned her to the sofa, strong body moulding round hers, kissing her until she was breathless, tickling her until she begged for mercy and promised that she would be properly respectful once on the boat.

Just the two of them, out on the sea. Anticipation quivered through every nerve. She was loving this slow sensual discovery but maybe it was time to take things to the next level. She pulled Akil down to her again, luxuriating in the weight of him, the strength of him, the sureness of his kiss. Today was going to be a very good day.

Akil knew that this thing with Clem couldn't last, and he was also all too aware that the closer they got, the harder their inevitable parting would be, but paradoxically he didn't care because every day they spent together he fell for her more and more.

He liked her frank, no-nonsense sense of humour. Enjoyed the conversation that flowed so easily between them. And he had never been so physically aware of a woman in his life.

Neither of them had discussed taking it slow, but somehow it felt right, learning each other bit by bit. It was tantalising in all the right ways. Especially as they were building up to something more; they both knew it. Awareness simmered between them as they got ready for their trip, every touch searing, every glance full of promise.

Before heading to the coast they stocked up on enough provisions to last them a week at sea. Shopping together should have been a mundane task, but it was a glimpse at a future that seemed infinitely desirable, if impossible, standing in a shop debating which cheese to select and what bread would go best with their choices, deciding if they wanted cakes or biscuits or both and how many raspberries were too many. They ended up laden with bags and baskets as they loaded up the car and set off to the harbour where he kept his boat.

'Oh, I like it here,' Clem exclaimed as Akil drove into the small car park at the harbour and parked up. 'This is where you brought me that first time—only this time we're Henri free.'

Akil slid out of the car and walked round to open the door. 'It must be a relief to have some time away from him. Lucky for you that I have secret service training.'

'Don't forget my black belt in karate.' Clem jumped out of the car and joined him at the back of the vehicle as he opened the catch and let the boot spring up. 'I have skills too.'

'That you do.' He swung the first of the picnic hampers out of the car, then more cautiously lifted out the second basket containing the drinks, setting it gently on the ground.

'I'll get these.' Clem reached in and pulled out the paper bags containing the fruit they'd chosen and the box of cakes. He kept crockery, cutlery, towels and cushions on board so all they'd needed to get was the food.

'You sure?'

'Well, fun as it would be for me to skip ahead while you stumble laden behind me, I can carry my share. You're meant to be advocating dismantling the patriarchy, re-member?'

'It's chivalry, not patriarchy,' he protested, and she laughed.

'Tell you what. I'll let you help me aboard.'

'It's my boat. I need to formally invite you anyway.'

'Like a vampire? Will I burst into flame if I put a foot aboard without a formal invitation? That must be an Asturian thing. I'm pretty sure we're not so formal in Cornwall.'

She gathered up the food and set off towards the harbour, Akil falling in beside her.

'I don't think poor Henri knows what to do with himself,' she said as they navigated the narrow path. 'He doesn't really do free time. I did point out to him that I look a lot more suspicious being shadowed by a six-foot-five rock of a man, but actually he does have this amazing ability to blend into the scenery. But he would literally give his life for Rosy so I guess that's a good thing. One less thing to worry about.'

'You worry about her?'

'She's going to be a queen one day. That's a tough gig. Of course I worry. I'm glad she has you as a friend though.'

They reached the small curve of the harbour and Akil exhaled as they stepped onto the jetty. It was a perfect sailing day. The sky was cloudless, the sea calm, the scent of salt and lemon permeating the air. He loved this moment of anticipation, the gorse-covered cliffs green behind him, the mountains rising majestically beyond, while turquoise seas stretched endlessly ahead. Here he wasn't the Vicomte d'Ortiz, carrier of his family's hopes and his father's thwarted ambitions. Here he wasn't a politician, a man who had put his own dreams aside. Here he was simply Akil. It was a rare pleasure.

Even rarer were the times he got to share this with someone. *Wanted* to share this with someone. And he had never brought a woman out to his boat before. Never wanted to share this most personal of pleasures. Never until now.

'Which is it?' Clem asked as they neared the end of the jetty. Most boats were moored further out, their dinghies bobbing off the jetty and harbour wall ready to ferry owners out. Akil reached his own dinghy and put the hampers at one end, before pointing out his boat.

'She's there.' He tried to keep the pride

out of his voice but knew he'd failed as Clem laughed.

'You sound like a proud father. Or husband.'

'She is the love of my life,' he admitted. He was only half joking. There were so few times when Akil felt really comfortable being himself, even when he was with his sister or with his fellow volunteers at the mountain rescue. He was always conscious of the image he projected, the weight of responsibility and expectation he carried. It was only out on the water where he could drop all his barriers. It was just a shame he rarely got to enjoy it.

'I can see why you're so proud, she is a beauty. Small but perfectly formed.'

'I didn't want the kind of superyacht I needed a crew for. Something small enough for me to manage myself, but big enough to take out to sea, to spend a week exploring the coast if I wanted.'

'Sounds idyllic.' The yearning in her voice was palpable. 'I've always wanted my own boat—but I could never justify the cost for the use I'd get from one. Not that I ever had the money even if I could justify it. Jobbing actress is not a lucrative profession and although I do have a trust fund it doesn't run to luxuries like keeping a boat. Do you get away often?'

'Not nearly enough. To be honest, I *can't* justify her really. She deserves more than the few days every now and then I can give her.'

'But you're here today.'

'We're here today. So let's make the most of it. Hop in.'

Clem stepped gracefully into the small inflatable tender and sat herself at the bow as Akil untied the rope and started the engine, steering the dinghy out towards where his boat was moored. She knew what she was doing, taking the rudder as he pulled alongside and secured the dinghy to the dock at the back and climbed aboard, extending a hand to help her up the ladder. She then helped him winch the dinghy up and secure it before turning around to survey his prized possession.

'Nice,' she said. 'Very nice.'

Akil wasn't being modest, the boat was compact with just one cabin although it had a comfortable double bed and plenty of storage. But the boat was perfect for him, combining swift, comfortable handling, with plenty of space on deck including seating, a built-in grill and bar and swimming platform while its size meant he could moor up in any port or cove he wished. With the sea literally within a second's access he had no need for the hot tubs or fancy fittings many of his peers enjoyed on their larger, more ostentatious vessels.

It didn't take long to give Clem the tour, and she was suitably appreciative, helping him stow away the provisions as she admired all the gadgets and clever use of space.

'Some of my friends' families have boats, small fishing boats or glorified dinghies, but nothing like this. She's in a class of her own. But I do know my way around a rope so set me to work.'

'In that case…' Akil motioned her towards the tiller. 'Do you want to take her out?'

'Really?' Her smile was all the reward he needed.

'Absolutely. Here, you turn this to get her started and the gears are here. Let me know if you need any help. I'll get the anchor.'

Akil's faith in Clem was justified as she expertly steered them towards the open sea. He leaned against the side and watched her as she confidently found a path through the buoys marking the way out. Her hair blew in the slight breeze, her eyes crinkling as she concentrated on the horizon, her poise strong and true.

She looked utterly beautiful, a sea naiad in her natural world. Akil's mouth dried. He'd never dared dream of being fully in sync with someone. Had never imagined it could be so easy spending time with another human, being himself. The irony of knowing it was temporary was not lost on him. But he pushed the thought aside. Akil knew how to make the best of things. How to snatch at moments of happiness while steadfastly doing his duty. This time wasn't any different.

'Which way shall I go?' Clem roused him from his thoughts and he straightened, joining her at the tiller.

'Up to you. Left will take us to the glitzy resorts just along the coast so head that way if you want cocktails and sophistication. It's quite a sight.'

'I'll bet. And what happens if I turn right?'

'Then you'll see tiny coves that can only be accessed by boat, isolation, stunning views, some of the best swimming you'll ever experience and an idyllic picnic spot.'

'Hmm, difficult decision.' She angled the

boat towards the right. 'How will I choose? The only thing…'

'Is?'

'I didn't come dressed for sailing, as you can see.' She flashed him a smile. 'Silk and lace are not really picnic attire but I can manage. But more crucially, I should have realised earlier when we were shopping, I don't have a bathing suit.'

Akil dropped a kiss onto her neck, his hand resting on the curve of her hip. 'Who said anything about costumes?'

Clem stilled. He could see her chest rise and fall as her breathing quickened, her cheeks and neck turned pink, her pupils dilated. He was so attuned to her every response, his own breathing sped up along with hers, heat rising throughout his body. When she finally spoke her voice was husky.

'I bet you say that to all the girls. Is this your routine? Invite a girl out for a sail and then suggest a dip but, oops, no costumes?'

'Not so far.' He paused, then said deliberately, 'You're the only woman I've ever invited abroad.'

She didn't respond, not at first, but he could see her work through the implications of that statement, before she turned and twined her arms around his neck, reaching up to press her mouth against his.

'What are we doing, Akil?' she half whispered, and he smoothed her hair back from her face.

'I don't know,' he said honestly. 'But we don't have to do anything, be anything. We can just sail or I can take us back. Just say the word.'

She shook her head emphatically. 'I don't want to go back,' she said, and he knew instinctively that she was talking about more than this trip.

'Then let's see where the wind takes us.'

She stared up at him, her eyes solemn and almost fearful until she seemed to shake her thoughts away, managing a smile as she turned back to the tiller. Akil leaned against her as she steered, his arm around her waist, holding her steady, wishing that she were someone less complicated, that he were someone without a predetermined path, that this could be the start of a longer voyage, the start of something real.

CHAPTER TEN

'THAT WAS A ridiculously delicious picnic.' Clem took another longing look at the leftovers before pushing her plate away with a groan. 'No. Don't let me eat any more. You might need to lose some ballast to get us back at the rate I've been consuming.'

She repressed a sigh at the thought of *back*. How she wished they could just sail on for ever. No worries about tomorrow, no family expectations—or in her case lack of family expectations—just the sea, a fair wind and each other. Because with Akil she was completely herself. Her hair was windblown, her skirt watermarked and her makeup non-existent and he didn't notice, didn't care. It was intoxicating.

'No more food. Got it. But we're now respectably heading towards evening so I could open the champagne and we can toast the view?'

It was a view worth toasting. Clem had kept hold of the tiller and taken them twenty miles up the rocky, dramatic coast where they'd moored up just inside a wide, deserted bay. They'd deliberated taking the tender in to picnic on the sandy beach but in the end elected to stay here on deck, the boat rocking gently with the tide.

'Champagne? Sounds good but should we drink and boat? I guess we could get Henri to pick us up at the other end.'

Akil leaned back in his seat and stretched and she did her best not to look at the tantalising glimpse of bared, muscled stomach. 'Of course, the best thing about a boat is that you don't have to worry about sailing under the influence, you can just stay where you are.'

Her whole body tingled at the thought. 'You mean just stay here? Overnight?'

'Here or further up the coast.' His eyes gleamed. 'There are many possibilities.'

'I see, so was this trip just a ruse, a plan to spirit me away like a pirate and sail away on the seven seas?' She was a very modern woman but she couldn't help but thrill at the thought. There *was* something piratical about Akil. He was usually so well put together, but here on the boat, the top few buttons of his shirt undone showcasing a tanned, muscular vee of chest, shirt sleeves rolled up to expose strong corded wrists, hair ruffled by the breeze, she could see traces of his warrior ancestors. Ancestors who might whisk an enemy princess away on their boat.

'Tempting.' His voice was husky, and it trembled through her, setting every nerve vibrating. 'But nothing so uncivilised.'

She held his gaze. 'Pity,' she said, and her stomach tumbled at his wolfish smile.

'You see,' he said, and it was as if he were undressing her with his eyes, 'I wouldn't want any woman who didn't want me with every part of her. Who I didn't want with every atom in me. And I do want you, Clem. So, what shall we do? It's up to you, it's always been up to you. Maybe you're the pirate...the pirate princess seducing the warrior into doing her bidding.'

His voice was hypnotic, low and mesmerising and she couldn't have moved if she'd tried. And she wasn't trying. Not when Akil was so close, the scent of him wrapping around her senses, making her dizzy with that intoxicating mix of salt and sandalwood. Not when her whole body buzzed with his proximity, her nerves alight, her legs weak and her breasts full, aching for a release so tantalisingly close.

She couldn't even speak, just quivered as he drew one finger along her cheek, brushing the tender outline of her mouth. 'Your move, Clem.'

No, she wanted to cry out. It wasn't fair, he couldn't leave this decision solely up to her, not when she instinctively knew that making love with Akil would make her more vulnerable than she had ever been before. Not when she needed reassurances and promises that this was right, that she was right. That *they* were right. That they had a future, even if that reassurance could only be a lie.

For a moment she desperately thought about changing the subject, backing away, even as her body cried out for her to just get on with it already. She was so close, so close to getting in too deep. Surely making love with Akil would tip her over the edge. If she wasn't there already and, oh, how she feared she might be.

But if she didn't she knew she would regret this moment of cowardice for the rest of her life. She wanted to know him fully, for him to know her. And besides, wasn't this where they had been heading since the day of the tour? More, since that very first meeting? Wasn't this what she craved, what she wanted more than air or water? If so, then how could she not?

More importantly, how could she not when he was allowing her to set the parameters, when he was putting her first? For a woman so often left in the shadows, that power was the most seductive thing of all.

'I have decided.' She stood up and faced him. No more thought. No more fears or doubts. Suddenly it was all very clear. She wanted Akil and he wanted her and that was all that mattered. 'I do want you. Here, to-night.'

It was his turn to stand, one hand on the boat rail, his gaze locked on her, his mouth curved into a wicked smile, one that sent shivers trembling through her. 'In that case, come here.'

He was now supremely arrogant, no longer the suave suitor or the sweet-tongued seducer. He was a man who knew what he wanted—*her*—and knew his goal was within reach. But she could match him, in desire, in need and in confidence that she was desired and needed in turn. The ultimate aphrodisiac. And, chin tilted, a sway in her step, fire consuming her, she stepped forward. Just one step.

'Now you.'

He raised an eyebrow, laughter lighting the darkness of his gaze as he casually stepped forward. But she wasn't fooled; for all his amusement there was a predatory air as he moved that showed his blood was up and he was fully focused on moving in for the finish. There was still space between them and he stared at her, daring her to complete it. Instead, Clem reached for her top button and, eyes fixed on him, flicked it open. She watched him swallow and allowed herself a feline grin.

'It's a little hot, don't you think?' Another button and then a third. 'Maybe we should cool off.' Another two and she slipped the blouse off her shoulders, her hands moving to the zip on her skirt. 'You did say this was a good swimming spot?' She stepped out of the skirt, leaving it pooled on the floor and, without looking away, undid the snap of her bra and let it fall away, feeling as much as hearing Akil's intake of breath as she did so. 'So, let's swim.' She kept her pants on, not quite ready to lose that last layer of protection as she stepped onto the swimming platform and pushed her hair back, looking back at him challengingly. 'Race you to the beach.'

It took Akil all of two seconds to react. He'd frozen in place while Clem discarded her clothes, unable to move a muscle as inch after delicious inch was bared, brown and lithe and delectable and—so it seemed—his. And then, just as he managed to wake up enough to reach for her she was gone, diving with clean precision into the sea and striking out for the beach. He allowed himself one lingering moment to take in the lines of her body forging through the water before tearing off his shirt and trousers and following her in.

The water was perfect, cool and refreshing, calm enough to make swimming a pleasure as Akil followed Clem, his blood up, closing in on his prey. Clem was a good swimmer, but he was better and he caught up with her with ease, then keeping pace alongside her until the water reached his chest at which point he stopped, reaching out to hook her and pull her close. Her hair, sleek with water, fell heavily around her shoulders, her chest rising and falling with exertion, water drying on her shoulders. She was all sea nymph, salt and water and flesh in a package he wanted to consume, like Poseidon claiming his prize. The water was deep enough to hide the rest of her body, but he knew just what was concealed, the high round breasts, a lighter shade than the rest of her olive body, the planes of her stomach and long, long legs, the triangle of silk that revealed as much as it concealed, now wet and translucent. Heat flooded him despite the chill of the water as he finally, finally, crushed her to him and took her mouth with his, not gently or sweetly but with a fierce possessiveness. A possessiveness she reciprocated. This was no coy naiad, rather a fierce and wild goddess as she wound her hands in his hair to pull him closer, her tongue entwined in his, hot and sweet, her breasts soft against his chest as he pulled her closer still.

Akil couldn't have said how long they stood, chest high in the waves, all he knew was that at some point he wanted, needed more, needed to touch as well as taste, needed to explore every inch of bared flesh. Slowly, unable to break the embrace, as if by doing so he might break the spell, he inched her back, back until the water receded, the sand soft under his feet, the early evening sun hot on his shoulders. But not as hot as the trail her hands blazed across his neck and down his back, not as hot as the flesh he skimmed as he finally, finally palmed one perfect breast, her damp skin silk under his touch. She inhaled sharply as his thumb reached her nipple, and he circled the tight bud slowly and with intent as he kissed his way down her jaw, down the proud slim column of her neck until he could replace his thumb with his mouth, cupping her other breast as he did so.

Blood surged triumphantly through his whole body, pooling at his groin, the urge to take her there and then almost overwhelming. *Steady*, he told himself. *Not yet.* He sank to his knees, pulling her with him, until she was supine on the sand beneath him, her beautiful body laid out like an offering, returning to her mouth as he straddled her.

Impatient, Clem pulled at him but Akil resisted with a low laugh, refusing to rush now that he had her here beneath him. Instead he concentrated on discovering every previously hidden inch, the places that made her gasp and buck and reach for him, holding onto his control with everything he had as his body clamoured for release.

'Now,' she whispered first softly and then impatiently but he resisted with painful restraint, pulling back to cup her face and kiss her with a melting slowness that almost undid him.

'Clem,' he murmured against her mouth. 'We need to return to the boat. I didn't get a chance to bring any protection.'

For one millisecond, Clem didn't care. For one moment she understood for the first time how desire and sensation could overwhelm common sense, but before she had time to act upon her instincts reality reasserted itself and she sat up, reluctantly, almost embarrassed by the abandon she'd displayed just moments before. 'Oh.'

'Oh, indeed. But I've seen you swim. I think we can be back on board in less than five minutes and carry on where we left off. What do you think?'

Again he was giving her the control, even though the evidence of his desire was all too visible, and that control only solidified her need. 'I think the quicker we get back, the better.' She allowed herself the luxury of running her eyes over him slowly and with intent, taking in every plane and hollow, every piece of hard sculpted flesh, and she could see him visibly shake with the effort of standing still as she caressed him with her gaze.

This time it was no mad dash, instead they kept pace with each other, knowing what awaited them at the return to the boat. Clem reached the ladder first and climbed, Akil right behind her. As soon as she was on the boat she turned, needing to kiss him, to hold him, to be held in turn. The water hadn't quenched her desire, instead the wait, the anticipation, had only stoked it and she pulled him close, entwining herself around him, until, with a muttered curse, he swept her up, laying her on the double sun lounger. She stayed still, drinking him in as he loomed above her.

'Don't move,' he ordered, and she obeyed, unable to do anything but wait, every nerve quivering, every sense greedily needy until he returned, tall and powerful and gloriously nude, a packet in his hands. He paused despite her whimpering protest and she felt his gaze wander over her as if he were touching her, her flesh goosepimpling under his study. 'You are beautiful,' he breathed. 'A sea goddess.'

'No more talking,' she managed and he laughed softly, sitting beside her.

'No? But I could write a poem to your eyes…' his finger brushed over them '…a sonnet to your mouth…' it moved lower still '…and a haiku about your neck. Your breasts deserve an ode.' She sucked in a breath as he lazily circled a nipple, replacing his finger with a tongue. 'Your stomach an elegy. And as for the soft skin here.' He moved his hand down to the tenderness of her inner thigh. 'Oh, I could write an epic poem about the way you feel here.'

She was panting now, her breasts rising and falling as need built inside her higher and higher, hotter and hotter. She'd never felt so wanted before, so desirable, so tempting. But then again no man had ever looked at her as if she were the answer to all his prayers.

And she had never wanted a man so fiercely either. The play of his muscles under her eager hands, the strength in his arms and chest, the tautness of his stomach. The way he hissed as her hand moved lower as he fought fire with fire, moving lower until he was kissing her stomach, her hips, her thighs, her inner thighs, his hand moving further up, knowing and sure.

'And here,' he whispered. 'Only a ballad would do for here.' Clem cried out, she couldn't fight back now, all thought disappearing under almost unbearable sensation until at last she broke, riding the wave again and again, exultant as he joined her, as if he were made for her, as if she were made for him.

Time ceased to have any meaning until she came to, wrapped around him, limp and sated, the stars shining down on them. Clem lay there, not knowing what to say or do. It had never felt like that before, never been as intense, as overwhelming. Part of her wanted to shout out in happiness, some part of her wanted to cry and, as if he understood, Akil rolled over to pull her closer, to envelop her in his arms.

'Are you okay?'

'Better than okay,' she reassured him, then, worried, 'You?'

His laugh rumbled through her. 'Better than okay.'

'Good, that's good.'

'It is.'

They lay there breathing in time until Akil sat up. 'I promised you champagne.'

'It's fine,' she reassured him, just wanting him back next to her but he was already on his feet.

'No, you should have champagne. We have the sound of the sea, we have the stars, we shouldn't waste it.'

'Well, if you insist.'

It took him less than two minutes to return with the chilled champagne and a bowl of the raspberries they'd bought earlier and, completely unselfconsciously, they stayed on deck, sipping and nibbling on the raspberries and talking nonsense as they gazed up at the stars. At some point, most of the champagne drunk, Akil kissed her once again and desire sprang back up as if they hadn't made love earlier, Clem responding with an ardency and urgency that would have surprised her if she'd had any room to think.

Later, much later, still under the stars but under a blanket Akil had brought up from the cabin, she began to fall asleep, safe in Akil's arms.

'I love you,' she murmured, so almost asleep she wasn't sure if she was imagining saying the words or not. Nor did she know if she imagined the pause that followed or the almost breathed response.

'*Je t'aime*, Clemence Beaumont. *Je t'aime.*'

CHAPTER ELEVEN

CLEM LAY BACK on the sunbed and breathed in. It was another hot, sunny day, the kind where she was glad to have little to do but swim and sleep. And she knew she needed to make the most of it, she wouldn't be able to stay in this idyll for much longer, nor enjoy almost guaranteed sun once she was back in the uncertainty of a UK summer.

Not that there was much summer left. She couldn't believe how quickly time had flown, but here she was facing the end of her stay. In less than a week she'd be returning to Cornwall and Arrosa would come home and start preparing for the ratification. She hadn't spoken to her sister for a couple of weeks, they'd just hurriedly exchanged a few messages, and she had no idea how she felt about returning to her normal life. Clem wasn't sure how she felt about her return to normality either.

On one hand, fun as being a tourist and enjoying the benefits of living in Arrosa's house were, she didn't think she was suited for a life without purpose. Sunbathing and swimming were fun, but she got just as much enjoyment out of the sessions at the hospital, more in fact, looking forward to the moment she sat down and transported the children away. After discussing it with Akil she'd started to do some research into what she'd need to do to qualify in occupational therapy and dramatherapy and had contacted a friend who worked in a theatre company that specialised in working with children in hospital and other non-home settings. She still had no concrete plans, but just having an idea of a path was a huge step forward.

But, of course, returning to Cornwall meant leaving Akil. And if that thought had been difficult *before* the trip out on the boat, it was almost unbearable now. She continued to see him nearly every day, although as summer drew to the end so his responsibilities grew, like a warning sign their time was nearly up. The need for discretion was as high as ever; the last thing either of them wanted was speculation about who Clem was or, worse, for people to start gossiping about how much time he spent at the palais with Arrosa. So she continued leaving the estate in one outfit and changing in a discreet location, and when they did venture out they mingled with tourists and sightseers far away from anywhere where Akil might meet friends or colleagues.

Clem wriggled again, trying to get comfortable. What had been fun at the beginning, an amusing subterfuge, was beginning to lose its charm. A reminder of why their relationship had to be secret, and that an end date was in sight. Fun as it was for them to lie in bed building castles in the air about a life sailing around Cornwall, she knew that leaving Asturia was not an option for him, just as staying was not an option for her. All she had ever wanted was someone to love her, to see her, to put her first. Ironic really that she had found someone who fitted the first two but couldn't fulfil the third.

At least neither of them had been foolish enough to mention love again. It didn't stop her thinking it though. Feeling it.

She closed her eyes, resolutely pushing the thoughts away although she knew that their reckoning was coming. They still had nearly a week. Maybe they would think of a solution before then. Maybe he'd ask her to stay, or she could suggest it. No one knew who she was. What did Clem Beaumont from England have to do with the royal family? Did he want more than a holiday romance? Did she? They had never discussed it.

She did her best to concentrate on the sensuous warmth of the sun across her body, the sound of the birds singing overhead and the distant drone of an aeroplane. Occasionally she heard voices from outside the villa gardens as the palais gardeners moved around, a burst of radio from one of the guards and his reply, footsteps coming down her path.

Hang on? *Footsteps.* Clem peeled her eyes open, suddenly alert. She wasn't expecting anybody. Akil was working this morning and nobody else ever came to see her. Feeling a little vulnerable in just her bikini, she sat up and grabbed her wrap, turning towards the path and the figure striding down it.

'There you are, Clemence.'

She blinked, myriad emotions whirlpooling through her, the way they always did on the rare occasions she saw her father, the less rare occasions she thought about him.

Sitting back, she peered over her sunglasses, deliberately cool and collected. 'Hello, Zorien. I wasn't expecting you. I must have missed your message.'

It was a long time since she'd called him *Daddy*; it had been made very clear to her that the word was not for her to use, not even in private, in case they were ever overheard. Safety trumped reality every time.

'You look well,' she added. 'Would you like to sit down? I'm sure I can manage some coffee.'

It had been several years since she'd last seen him, but he looked exactly the same, tall, slim and straight-backed, his hair not yet silvering. The hazel eyes so similar to hers and Arrosa's were cool and assessing, his expression inscrutable.

'Your sister stands when I first enter a room, curtseys, says *Your Majesty* and waits for me to speak.'

It was like that, was it? Clem smiled, affecting an insouciance she didn't feel. 'I missed the day my local comprehensive taught court manners. But on the other hand, we're outside so this isn't actually a room and you're not *My* Majesty. I'm not an Asturian citizen, remember?'

One of many points of contention. Zorien wasn't named on her birth certificate so she had no claim to citizenship although thanks to her mother she held French as well as British citizenship.

'But any guard or member of staff could see you not adhering to protocol. You should know better than to let your guard down, Clemence.'

'No one's looking. Besides, what will they do? Arrest me for lack of courtesy and take me to the tower?'

'You are always so argumentative, Clemence.' The first time they'd met in years and already they were at odds, the same old pattern. It was like the time he'd come to see her on her eighteenth birthday, and they had managed about fifteen minutes before she'd crashed out of the house in a rage, angry that he wouldn't be there for her last school play, one she had helped direct as well as starred in, a labour of love she had wanted to share with both her parents. Angry that he wouldn't even come for a walk with her in case they were seen. Angry that he'd refused her request to spend the summer in

Asturia. She'd said bitter words, a lifetime of resentment and hurt spilling out, and in the end he had simply walked away. Soon after he'd made it clear it was no longer safe for Arrosa to spend her summers in Cornwall.

Their relationship had never really recovered; it had never had the opportunity. It wasn't as if they ever spent time together to repair it, his calls infrequent, his visits even more so.

Zorien Artega had done his duty materially. Her trust fund had been set up before she was born, more money was deposited in her account every birthday and Christmas and upon her mother's death she'd found out the house had been held in trust for her. There were times when she'd wanted to throw her trust fund back at him, to tell him that she needed nothing from him. But without it she had nothing. No family, no security net, no proof of who she was and that anyone had ever cared about her.

But he was here now, and this was what she had wanted, had hoped for. She couldn't allow her temper and age-old hurt to get in the way. 'I'm going to make coffee,' she said in as conciliatory a manner as she could manage. 'Sure you don't want some?'

He continued to survey her for another long moment, then nodded. 'Coffee would be nice.'

They didn't speak again until Clem had set the coffee pot onto the table, quickly ducking into the bedroom and throwing a dress over her bikini and pulling a comb through her hair. After a moment's hesitation she added a wrap, a dash of lipstick and some mascara. It wasn't that she wanted to impress her father, but she did want the protection of respectability. She returned to the kitchen, pouring the milk into a jug and tipping some biscuits onto a plate, carrying the lot outside. She took a seat opposite him and handed him a cup.

'It's beautiful here. I always thought the house in Cornwall the most perfect setting, and I do like to be beside the sea, but if I can't have the sea then a lake is certainly a good substitute.'

'Your sister seems happy here,' Zorien said. 'I had my doubts when she wanted to move out of her apartments in the palais, but this seemed like a good compromise. She is still protected by the palais guards, still looked after by the staff but she has some independence.'

Some was the relevant word here; Clem knew her sister's comings and goings were recorded and scrutinised but it was a compromise Arrosa had made and it wasn't for her to comment.

Zorien sipped his coffee then set his cup down. 'How are you, Clem? It can't have been easy for you the last few months.'

'I'm fine,' she said as brightly as she could. 'Aren't I always? Stay out of trouble and need nothing, that's my role.'

But he didn't rise to the bait, looking her over with eyes that were suddenly kind, and she blinked; kindness was almost more than she could bear. 'You shouldn't have had to deal with your mother's illness alone,' he said. 'I'm more sorry about that than you can know.'

'The nurses you paid for were more than helpful.' The least she could do was give credit where credit was due. 'And Maman loved the gifts you sent. You always seemed to know what would cheer her up.' Every day something new would arrive, her mother's favourite flowers, gloriously soft cashmere socks and wraps, fresh baskets of fruit, luxury creams and lotions, delicate cakes to tempt a disappearing appetite.

'I should have been there, come to see her before the end. I think…' For a brief second, he looked vulnerable. 'I think I was in denial; your mother was so full of life it seemed impossible that life could be cut short. If anyone could beat a diagnosis like hers, I thought she would.'

There were so many things Clem could respond with. She could point out that if he had been there, if he'd seen her mother, he'd have known how ill she was, that those who cared for her day to day didn't have the luxury of dreaming that everything was going to be okay. But what was the point? 'I think we all hoped that,' she said instead.

Silence fell once again, thoughts of her mother permeating the air around them. She was the link, their common ground, the woman they both had loved. Now she was gone, was anything left in their relationship to salvage? Did her father even want to salvage it? Would it be far more convenient for him if Clem disappeared never to be seen again?

'You seem to have been very busy while you have been here,' he said at last.

Clem looked at him warily, but he seemed to be genuine. 'I've heard good reports about the impact your reading is having at the hospital. It's kind of you to give up your time. It's the sort of thing I could imagine your mother doing.'

'I kind of fell into it really, but I am enjoying it.'

'Will you continue when you go back?'

When you go back: there was clearly no doubt in her father's mind that her stay here was temporary. 'Possibly,' she conceded. 'I've been wondering what to do with my life. Taking eighteen months out has changed everything. Acting doesn't seem like the be-all and end-all any more. Doesn't seem as important as it once did. I've been thinking about maybe retraining, looking at something like occupational therapy. It's early days, I don't want to rush into anything, but it might be a rewarding thing to do.' She paused, hating how much she wanted his opinion, his approbation, but she could feel his approval warming her through as he slowly nodded.

'That sounds like a good plan. You'd be good at that.'

'Thank you.'

'I've also heard,' he continued, and something in the way he shifted told Clem that this was the purpose of the meeting. He wasn't here to catch up with her, nor to compliment her on her work at the hospital, he was here to deliver a message. She straightened and met his gaze coolly, glad of the lipstick and combed hair. 'That you've been spending a great deal of time with the Ortiz heir.'

'Akil? Yes, he's been very kind.'

'The pair of you have been very discreet and I appreciate that, but he's a young man on the rise and the press will start to take notice sooner rather than later. Will want to know who you are.'

'All they would find out is that I'm an English actress here on holiday.' She knew she sounded defensive and tried to rein it in. 'There is nothing to link me to you. That's what you're worried about, isn't it?'

'You are staying in my home, accompanied by your sister's bodyguard, there's a link. It would take one enterprising journalist to work that out. But there's more, Clem. Your behaviour is rousing suspicion. People are wondering where Arrosa is every day. She sets off for Court but no one sees her. I have put off any queries, as far as anyone knows she's with me, but people won't really believe she's shut up in my private apartments all day every day. It's stretching credulity. The gate logs from here come to me, but they also go to the Army General. They show Arrosa as coming back late or not coming back at all. Sooner or later, this will leak, people will wonder where she is, what she's doing.'

Heat flooded her cheeks; to think she'd been congratulating herself how discreet she and Akil had been. Of course her behaviour would be noticed and reported on, no matter what she, Akil and Henri did to mitigate it. And now her father was having to cover for her and Akil.

'I'll be more careful. I'm leaving soon anyway.' But she knew that wasn't the right answer. He wasn't here to ask her to be more discreet, he was telling her to stop seeing Akil.

Zorien leaned forward and although his eyes were kind, they were also implacable. 'You've done a good thing, Clem. Your sister needed time away and you made that happen. But when she returns, things are going to get more and more intense. Her life was difficult as my only child.'

Clem did her best not to wince at his

words. *Only child.* That put her very firmly in her place.

'It's been very difficult as we have worked to change the law, especially as I know she has no real desire to be Queen and part of her would have been happy leaving things as they were. But nothing can really prepare her for what life will be like in just a few weeks when she officially becomes my heir. Everything she says, everything she does, will be under intense scrutiny, at home and internationally. She has to show that she is fit to rule, that she has what it takes to manage this country. Everything we do needs to support that. Do you understand what I'm saying?'

'Yes. I understand, I've never done anything but understand. Asturia comes first, I come second. That's how it's always been, isn't it, Zorien?'

He shook his head. 'Not you, Clem. *Us.* We Artegas. Asturia comes first, the family second. We are the servants of this country, and we can never forget it.'

'But it's *not* my country. That's been made very clear to me.'

'But you're here, and you love it, don't you? You've explored the mountains, the villages, and the seas. You've spent time in hospitals, eating our food, walking our streets, exploring our heritage—your heritage. Don't think that I don't know that the sacrifice you make is greater in some ways than the sacrifices your sister and I have to make.'

'But you have each other.' She hated the tears filling her eyes, the wobble in her voice. 'I have no one.' No one but Akil— and she had known she would need to say goodbye, she had just hoped for more time.

'Please don't think that I don't want to be more involved in your life, and I know Arrosa wishes she could be a proper sister to you. But this is what we do, all of us, and you have your part to play as well. The last thing we need right now is the publicity that would surround us if there was any suspicion of who you really are. I'm glad you had a chance to be here, to get to know the country, but it's time for you and Arrosa to resume your normal lives. Your life is in England, Clem. That's what your mother chose for you.'

'But what if that's not what I want?'

'What we want is secondary to what we need to do. Look at you, Clem, you're an Artega through and through. Our blood into your veins and I know I can trust you to do what's right. You've given your sister the space she needed to prepare for her future, to grow into her role. Your plans for your future sound exciting, and I will help in any way I can.'

'As long as I pursue them away from here?'

Her father nodded. 'The last year and a half have been difficult for you, and you deserved some fun, but it's time for the fun to stop. I'm sorry, Clem. I wish it could be different, but it's time you went home.'

It wasn't like Clem not to reply to his messages, but a couple of hours after letting her know he was free, Akil had still not heard from her, nor was she at the hospital. He had tried to be discreet about visiting her at the Palais d'Artega, not wanting his presence there too often to be noted, but when his third call went to voicemail his worry intensified and he headed out towards the country estate, discretion the last thing on his mind.

It wasn't just that it was unlike her to go AWOL. He needed to see her. It had been hard to settle to work that morning; every hour that passed was a reminder that summer was nearly over, and Clem would be returning to England soon. It had been easy to ignore that realisation; when they had started to get close, summer had seemed endless. Besides, they had both known the score. Theirs was just a holiday fling, some fun while Clem was in Asturia.

But what they had was stronger, deeper, than a fling. And now, as every day got dark a little earlier and the noonday sun sank a little lower, reality was setting in. He loved her.

The irony didn't escape him; he was a man who didn't really believe in love and certainly didn't believe in love at first sight, but he couldn't deny that something in him had shifted the very first time they'd met. He'd grown up to think of love as weakness, as destructive, but being with Clem just made him stronger. Talking to her, listening to her, finding out her perspective made him a better politician, a more strategic thinker—look at his plans for the hospital inspired by her. Was she the politician's wife of his dreams? No, but he was very glad he hadn't met the well-connected and diplomatic hostess he'd thought he wanted to marry. He needed someone to challenge him, someone to complement him. Love wasn't weakness, as he had feared, but strength, allowing himself vulnerability in front of another human being.

And he was sure that she needed him, too. For all her strength she needed to be loved, to be needed; she'd been alone too long. Which was why Akil was going to ask her to stay in Asturia. To stay with him. A smile curved his mouth at the thought of evenings curled up and days out exploring, of long nights loving and laughing. It was more than he'd ever thought he'd have and now it was within his grasp. How could one person change everything so completely?

He'd known since the first night on the boat that he couldn't just let her leave, but now time was running out and he still hadn't found the right time or words. He'd even considered proposing, but his natural caution urged him against making such an irrevocable move just yet. After all, his parents' marriage stemmed from a summer romance gone wrong, and he didn't want to repeat that mistake. He and Clem needed to spend every season together before making such a commitment. But he was looking forward to every one of those seasons.

He knew it wouldn't be easy. Even if she were just an English tourist here for the summer then there would still be some obstacles to overcome. Her life was overseas, she had no job here, and his work and the obligations of his title were both demanding. But she wasn't just an English tourist, she was the illegitimate daughter of the King, and from everything she'd told him he knew Zorien and those court officials who knew of her existence would not welcome her presence in Asturia full-time. But they couldn't let that stop them. If she wanted to stay, they would find a way to make it work.

By the time he reached the Palais d'Artega he'd still not heard from her, and tension gripped him as he turned in through the gates. As usual he was waved through but, this time, he was aware of some curious glances from the usually inscrutable guards and knew that he wouldn't be able to visit her here again. If his presence here was being noted, it had to stop.

As he drove along the formal driveway another car was coming the other way and Akil slowed and pulled in to allow it to pass. As it drew close, Akil saw Zorien at the wheel, his expression dark and filled with pain. His gaze met Akil's and he nodded curtly. Akil's pulse began to hammer as he noted what looked like pity in the King's eyes and the feeling of tension increased as he sped a little faster than usual past the palais and out towards the villa.

He pulled up outside and jumped out of his car, making his way around to the back of the house, instinctively knowing that Clem would be standing by the lake. He knew at times of stress she gravitated towards water and sure enough she was standing on the platform where he had first seen her, wearing a long green sundress that fell around her ankles. Her head was bent but she looked up as he approached, and he saw her eyes were red. Her father had made her cry.

He clenched his fists; he knew better than anyone that family relationships were complicated, but Clem had nobody. Surely Zorien understood that? Would it have cost him to be kind?

'Hi,' she said, her voice a little husky.

'I'm glad you're okay. I got a little worried when I didn't hear from you.'

'Sorry, my father was here. I haven't had a chance to check my phone.'

'I saw him on the way out. I'm glad he managed to visit you. How was it?'

Her smile was tremulous. 'As expected. He's given me my marching orders.'

Anger and possessiveness rose in him, almost overwhelming as he strode forward to take her hands. 'He can't do that.'

'He's the King. I'm pretty sure he can do anything he likes.'

'We're a democracy and you're of age. You can do anything you want, Clem.'

She pulled her hands away and tried another smile. 'What does it matter, Akil? We knew this day was coming, it's just a little earlier than expected. This was only a summer fling.'

He took her shoulders and looked down at her defiant face. 'Is that really true, Clem? Because it isn't for me. I love you—and I think that you love me.'

CHAPTER TWELVE

Clem stared up at Akil, her eyes filling with unwanted tears. She tried to blink them back, not wanting to show any sign of weakness. 'Love is a big word, Akil.'

'It's not one I use lightly.' His voice was teasing, warm, but his face was full of concern—for her.

She twisted away, not sure she'd be able to do what had to be done if he was touching her. 'Say I was falling in love with you, what difference would it make? My life is far away from here, and there's nothing for you in Cornwall.'

'Apart from you.'

She closed her eyes, trying to regain control of her voice. 'But I wouldn't be enough. We both know that. You have your role here, your title, the promise you made to your father. You couldn't give that up for me.' Although a selfish part of her wished he could.

'No, maybe not long term, although I'd love to visit your home,' he conceded. 'But, Clem, you could stay. You could extend your role at the hospital; we could look into funding to make it a real job if that's what you wanted.'

'And what? Live with you?'

'Why not?'

'Because I don't belong here. I'm not wanted here.'

'I want you, and I bet your sister does too.'

She knew he was trying to help but how she wished he wouldn't; every word just made it worse, showing her a future she could never inhabit. 'My mother left France because it was considered too close to Asturia, too risky. At one point my father tried to persuade her that she should move to New Zealand in order to protect the secret of my existence, but she didn't want to go so far alone so they compromised on Cornwall. I don't think, judging on the conversation we've just had, that he's changed his mind.'

'This isn't about him.'

'No, it's about me. He reminded me that if word got out about who I was then life will be even more difficult for Rosy—and it's going to be hard enough for her from now on, we both know that. I love my sister, Akil, she is the one constant I have. I couldn't live knowing my existence was like some time bomb waiting to explode.'

'Have you asked her? Because I bet you anything she would tell you that she doesn't care about any possible scandal, that she would give anything to have you close by. She loves you too, Clem. She would want you to be happy.'

'But how could I be happy living so close to a father and sister who can't acknowledge me? If you and I were together then wouldn't there be times we were in the same place and at the same events? And we would have to be strangers! I can't live like that, I can't. I can't be here unacknowledged, unwanted. It would break me, Akil.' The words were torn from her, and the tears she so desperately tried to keep back made it through the barriers. 'How could I live as a stranger to my family?'

He enfolded her in his arms, and she allowed herself the luxury of leaning in against him. 'You're not unwanted, Clem. Never that. I'd be by your side throughout.'

How she wished she could believe him. 'And if we didn't work out? We barely know each other after all, it's just been a few weeks. You're the one who said that mutual goals were a better basis for a relationship than love. That love complicates things, that your parents married as a result of a summer romance and made each other miserable. What if that is us? What if we realised in a week, or a month or a year that it wasn't working? Where would I be then? Surely it's better to make a clean break before we're in too deep?' She allowed herself another second of absorbing his strength, memorising every muscle, before she stepped back, trying to keep her expression neutral, to hide how much every word hurt.

'I did say that.' His smile was rueful. 'And I meant it. But that was because I didn't know what love was. I'd never been in love before, you see. I do know now, though, thanks to you, Clem, and my feelings aren't going to change. You just need to trust me.'

'I can't. I can't, Akil. I wish I could. It's a nice idea, extending whatever this is between us, but it's not practical. Better to realise that what we have here is a summer romance, a lovely, memorable time out from reality. I'll always cherish it.'

'Or maybe it's more, maybe we have the chance of something extraordinary.'

'Maybe in another life.'

'We only get this one chance, Clem.'

'I'm sorry,' she whispered, not able to prolong the torture for another moment. 'But you have to go. I need to pack.'

Akil stood stock-still, dark eyes blazing. 'Don't just give up on us, Clem. Don't give in without a fight.' He stared at her for a moment longer and, unable to bear the weight of his gaze, she looked away. By the time she looked back, he was gone.

Clem stood frozen to the spot for one moment and then sank to her knees, letting out a howl of such grief it shocked her, and then another one wracking her body. She crouched there, allowing the tears to flow and the sobs to pour out until she was spent with emotion, and then clambered to her feet. Her chest and throat ached, but the pain in her chest, which had tightened the whole time Akil had been here, was gone. Now she could move.

Her father had arranged for the plane to

fly her back that evening, so she headed back up the garden to the villa mechanically. She'd brought very little with her, so as not to arouse suspicion, and it didn't take long to put her scant few belongings in her bag. A paper bag on the dressing table held the bracelets and cufflinks she'd bought a few weeks ago and she slipped one bangle onto her wrist, leaving the other for her sister. She held the cufflinks tight in her hand for one long moment then slipped them into her pocket—she'd ask Henri to deliver them. Her bag packed, she took it through to the hallway and then began to tidy up the coffee she'd made earlier.

She needed to keep busy. She couldn't allow herself to think, to feel, to understand that this was her last day in Asturia, that she'd never see Akil again, had no idea when she'd see her sister again.

Finally, there was nothing else to do and Clem wandered back out into the garden and down to the bathing platform staring out at the lake, at the magnificent palais in the distance. She'd never wanted to grow up here; beautiful as it was, she preferred the Cornish cottage, and was immensely grateful she'd not had to deal with all the rigmarole and ceremonial nonsense Arrosa had had to navigate. But she'd like to have been able to visit here, to share this house with her sister, for them to be sitting here by the lake together gossiping, a chilled bottle of wine awaiting them on the terrace.

If she'd said yes to Akil, if she'd been braver, stronger, would that have been a possibility? How could it have been? She and Rosy could have no public relationship; that was why she had to go home, for her sister.

Clem sat down and trailed her hand in the cold water, closing her eyes and remembering the moment Akil had kissed her in the sea, the overwhelming sensations. It had all been overwhelming. Yes, she wanted to protect her sister, but she also needed to protect herself. She was frightened of being hurt, frightened of being left behind, frightened of not being enough.

But it was too late. She had let Akil into her heart and now she was hurting, more than she'd ever imagined possible. But it wasn't Akil's fault; she was doing it to herself. He wanted her to stay; he wanted her to be with him. She was the one turning away.

She knelt down and stared at her reflection in the water, pale and big eyed. What if she did stay? What was the worst that could happen? She couldn't control what her father did or said, and she'd have to be respectful of Arrosa's wishes around any kind of public relationship, but really who would connect Clemence Beaumont with the royal family? Her similarity to her sister was striking, but wild dark curls and hazel eyes were common enough in Asturia.

Akil loved her. She rocked back as the truth of the words hit her. What must it have cost him to have said that? To have made himself so vulnerable, he who lived a life led by duty and responsibility? But he loved her and wanted her no matter the consequences. It was what she'd always wanted and yet she was willing to throw it away.

How could she when she loved him? Could she really return home and carry on living without him? Carry on as if all this had never happened? Of course she couldn't. She was no longer that grieving girl with no idea who she was and what she wanted, who had arrived here just a few weeks before. Akil had helped her find the way. And her way was with him.

She just had to find a way to tell him.

* * *

Akil didn't know where he was going to go or what he was going to do as he drove away from the Palais d'Artega, but one thing he did know for sure. This was *not* the end of the conversation. He was not going to just give up.

It would be one thing if Clem had decided to go back to Cornwall of her own volition; if she didn't care enough about him to stay. He wasn't going to pretend that it wouldn't hurt, but he'd have to accept her decision. But he was pretty sure that was not what was going on here. He had no idea exactly what Zorien had said to her but whatever it was had clearly persuaded her that she had no place in Asturia, that her very presence was a danger to her sister.

But the real danger was the secret itself. Secrets had power, a power that only existed as long as the secret did, a power that disappeared once freed. Clem was in her twenties now, and Zorien had technically been a free man when she'd been conceived. The news of her existence would undoubtably cause some scandal, but it would be a short-lived one, especially if both the Artega and the Ortiz families rallied around her.

But what could Akil do? It wasn't his secret to spill, his call to make.

Before he could think better of it, he tapped the call button on his dashboard and commanded his phone to call Arrosa. It rang several times before she picked up.

'Akil, is everything okay?'

'Not exactly. Have you spoken to your father?'

'Funny you should ask that. He's left me a voicemail and a couple of messages, telling me it's time to come home.' He couldn't quite tell what the Princess thought of her father's command.

'He's told Clem the same thing, that her time here is up,' he said grimly.

'I guess we always knew it wasn't for ever,' Arrosa said, a shadow of unhappiness in her voice.

'You certainly couldn't keep this pretence up for ever. At some point people will want to see the Princess's face,' Akil said dryly. 'Clem needs to be able to leave the palais without disguises and subterfuge. But that doesn't mean that things should have to go back to the way they were. Don't you agree?'

There was a startled silence at the end of

the phone. 'What do you mean?' she asked at last.

'We're about to begin a new era here in Asturia, spearheaded by you, Arrosa. Don't you think it's time for a new start in every way?'

'Is this about Clem?'

'I love her,' he said deliberately. 'And I think that she loves me, but she won't stay here with me, she won't put her happiness first, because your father has told her that if anyone finds out who she is the scandal would be too much for you and she loves you too much to be a burden to you.'

'But that's not it at all, Akil. I would love everyone to know who she is, I am so proud of her, but how could I do that to her? Clem has never been the target of the press. She's never been followed anywhere, she's never been commented on, she's never had her outfits dissected, her love life speculated on, her every expression misinterpreted until she had to learn to show no expression at all. She has a freedom that I can never have, and that freedom is the greatest gift I can give her. If anyone knew who she was, she'd lose that.'

'I think that should be her decision, don't you? Arrosa, don't you see, you're protecting her and she's protecting you and the only people losing out are the two of you?'

'And this is all altruistic on your part?'

'I don't deny that I would like her to stay in Asturia, that I would like to carry on seeing her, but this is beyond us, whatever we are. She is all alone, Arrosa. She is going back to Cornwall with no family, no one who really cares about her apart from you and me.'

There was another long silence before she asked, 'What do you want me to do?'

'I'm going to go see your father to tell him that I think he should come out and acknowledge her if that's what she wants. And then I am going to see if I can persuade your stubborn sister to give us a chance. I just need to know; will you back me up or not?'

'If that's what Clem wants, then yes. I will.'

'Thank you, that's all I needed.'

Akil said goodbye then hung up, and headed towards the castle, parking in his usual spot just outside parliament, and striding into the building, flashing his pass at every barrier and guard post until he'd reached the doorway that separated the royal apartments from the parliamentary building. There he was forced to halt and give his name to a footman and request a meeting with Zorien.

'He'll see me,' he said with a certainty that made the footman look taken aback. Sure enough, the man was back within minutes.

'He said to bring you straight in,' he said in obvious surprise. 'Follow me.' He led Akil through several corridors until they finally reached the heavy oak door that barred the way to Zorien's private office. The footman knocked and opened it, gesturing for Akil to go in.

The King stood at the window gazing out, turning as Akil walked towards him and made a swift bow. 'I was wondering if I'd see you today,' he said.

'Your Majesty.' He straightened. 'I think you know why I'm here.'

Zorien gestured towards a chair. 'Sit down, d'Ortiz. Brandy? No? You're sure?' He sat opposite Akil and sighed. 'It's for her own good, you know,' he said. 'For both their good.'

Akil made himself consider every word, use his politician's diplomacy, not the righteous anger that rumbled through him. 'Isn't that their decision to make now? They're not children any more, Your Majesty. They are women, strong women who have been through a great deal in different ways. They need each other, want to support each other as the sisters they are. It should be their choice where Clem lives and whether they see each other, not yours.'

'So this is an intervention on their behalf? I think both my daughters are capable of speaking for themselves.'

'So do I. But thanks to you they both think silence benefits the other. I don't know if that is deliberate manipulation or an unfortunate misunderstanding, but while they both think they are doing what's best for the other they are not going to challenge you. I, on the other hand, have no such scruples. Instead, I wanted to give you fair warning.' Akil held the King's gaze. 'I love Clem, I want to make a life with her, and I don't care whether you are happy for her to stay in Asturia or not. But *she* cares and that matters to me.'

'So you're here for my blessing.'

'I don't need anyone's blessing. But Clem does. She needs to know that you love her, that you care about her, that you want her in your life. And you should want her. She's an amazing woman, kind and intelligent—and she tells it how it is, which is a really rare quality. She could be a real asset to you, and a real asset to Arrosa. But that's not why you should acknowledge her. You should do it because it's the right thing to do. Because she has nobody else, and you are her father.'

'And you think it's as easy as that, do you?'

Akil smiled at that. 'You and I both know that in politics the easiest decision is rarely the right one. Of course it won't be easy. There will be a lot of talk and a lot of speculation, and it will be unpleasant for a while.'

'I have a wife who is innocent in all this.'

'And a daughter who is also innocent. Clem deserves to hear you stand up for her, for you to say publicly that you're proud of her. Whether you do so is up to you. It's not up to me to spill your secrets. But it's not for me to hide them either. I am going to do everything in my power to persuade Clem to make a life with me here whether you like it or not. And if I do then you will have to find a way to live with that that makes her happy—because if I see you snub her even once, if I ever see her look the way she looked after your visit today again, then this won't be such a civilised conversation.'

'You've made yourself very clear, d'Ortiz.'

'Good.'

The King sighed. 'Are you sure you don't want a drink? I think I need one.' He stood up and poured two generous measures of brandy, setting one before Akil. 'I have to say, I am half hoping she turns you down. You would be an exhausting son-in-law. But maybe it would be better to have you close. You could also be an asset as Arrosa starts to take the reins. A brother-in-law like you on her side would be a formidable weapon.'

'As would Clem, if she has a place here. You'll consider it?'

'I need to talk to Arrosa and I need to talk to my wife, but if Clem wants me to publicly recognise her, then maybe it's time. Tell her I will think about it.'

Akil stood up, his brandy untouched. 'Thank you, sir.'

'Good luck, d'Ortiz.'

Akil grinned then. 'I'll need it. Your daughter can be very stubborn, sir.'

'Don't I know it. She's very like her mother.' The rather austere face softened. 'I did what I thought was right at the time, what I thought was right for Asturia, and I don't do regrets. Iara has been a good queen, maybe better than I deserve, and I love my daughter more than she'll ever know. But I wish I could have been a father to Clem, shown her how proud I am of her.'

'It's not too late, sir.' Akil just hoped it wasn't too late for him as well. But he came from a long line of warriors. It was time to fight.

CHAPTER THIRTEEN

CLEM TURNED AWAY from the lake and marched back up to the villa full of purpose. As she reached the terrace she saw a tall figure waiting for her. Her heart leapt, only to sink again when she realised it was Henri; his usually impassive face was full of sympathy.

'The plane is waiting for you, Your Highness.'

'Henri, you really don't have to *Your Highness* me. You never did. I'm just Clem,' she said, and a smile crinkled the usually austere face.

'No matter what, you're the King's daughter, and you deserve the title.'

'Thank you. I'm glad Rosy has you to look out for her. Just let me get my things.'

Clem collected her bag and jacket then stood in the hallway looking around for a moment, picturing her sister working at the desk in the study, stirring something on the stovetop, relaxing in front of the TV. If things went the way Clem hoped, would she be here with her sometimes?

'This isn't goodbye,' she said. 'But *au revoir*, I hope.'

She cast one look around and then followed Henri out to the car, waiting until he opened the door and ushered her inside. As he settled himself inside the driver's seat she leaned forward.

'Henri, will you do me a favour?'

'You look just like your sister when you ask that,' he said suspiciously. She smiled.

'Can we go via the beach? You remember the beach I went to with Akil that first week? I just want to walk on the beach one last time, see the sea so I can remember it.'

She crossed her fingers, hoping that Henri wouldn't point out that she lived by the beach and could see the sea any time she wanted, but simply nodded as he turned on the engine. Clem sat back and pulled her phone out of her bag, typing a brief message.

I'm on the beach. Can we talk?

It wasn't a long drive, but Clem looked out and learnt every piece of it by heart as she pondered the conversation that awaited her—if Akil showed up. She knew one thing: she couldn't allow her future to be decided by Akil. If for whatever reason he changed his mind, if he decided that he'd been right all along and that love was too messy and unpredictable, if he decided he wanted that diplomatic polite marriage after all, she couldn't blame him, nor could she use that as an excuse to run home and hide from the consequences of her decisions.

She had to decide whether Asturia was part of her future or not, not Akil. She had to set the boundaries for any future relationship with her family, not him. She'd been passive long enough. It was time she came out of the shadows. Of course she wanted Akil by her side when she did, but thanks to him she was strong enough to do it alone if she had to.

She just hoped she didn't.

It was mid-afternoon by the time they reached the beach and the car park was busier than she'd seen it, families unloading picnics and groups of teens with surfboards. Many stopped to stare curiously at the limousine.

'Don't open the door for me, Henri,' Clem asked as he pulled the handbrake. 'I don't think anybody will mistake me for my sister, but if they see you acting all chauffeur-ish someone might put two and two together and make six.'

Sure enough, although a few people stared at her as she opened the door and slid out, no eyes widened with recognition and no one showed any sign of being interested in taking her photo or speaking to her. How different it must be for her sister, not able to even have a simple walk on the beach without Henri's presence to keep onlookers away. If Akil was right, if her sister was prepared to risk scandal and have Clem close by, then was Clem prepared to be the scandal? To be stared at and whispered about and photographed?

With her sister and Akil by her side, she could weather anything.

Clem slipped off her shoes and walked barefoot onto the beach, heading towards the shoreline where gentle waves lapped the sand, holding up her skirt so she could wade in up to her ankles, tipping her head up to look at the sky, the same deep blue as the sea. How she loved the smell of sea air, the salt and water and air combining into something more than the sum of its parts. It smelt like home. She could live anywhere as long as she could feel sand beneath her toes and submerge herself in the sea.

She checked her phone, there was no message, no answer from Akil, but there was a brief message from her sister.

I just want to say that whatever you do decide I have your back, always. I'm proud of you and I'm proud to have you in my life and I am happy to shout it from the rooftops to anyone and everyone if that's what you want. I love you, big sis.

Clem swallowed. She'd cried more than enough today, but it was hard to read the message through blurry tears. She quickly sent a reply.

Right back atcha!

Casting a hopeful look back towards the harbour, Clem continued her slow wade through the soft surf feeling freer than she had done for longer than she could remember. Free of worries, free of insecurities, free to be herself whoever and whatever that meant.

Without allowing herself to think what she was doing, she headed back to the beach and pulled her dress over her head, wrapping her phone in it and laying them on her shoes, and then she turned to wade right back in, heading out until she was waist deep and then diving into the waves, submerging herself, letting the water wash away the last of the doubt and the insecurity. Not the grief; that would never quite go, but with time she would learn to manage it.

As Akil left the castle his phone buzzed and his heart rate sped up, only to decrease when he realised it was from Arrosa.

Whatever Clem wants, whatever Clem decides, I will always back her.

He inhaled, relief filling him. He didn't necessarily need the Princess on his side, but he did need her on Clem's. He replied quickly.

Thank you. I've just had an interesting conversation with your father, I think we've reached a similar consensus.

He sent the message and jammed the phone back into his pocket as he reached the car, unlocking it and sitting behind the wheel trying to decide where he should go, what he should do. In one way nothing had changed since he had left Clem and yet at the same time everything had changed. He understood her position a little bit better, thanks to his conversations with Arrosa and with the King, and he knew that he could promise with truth that if Clem decided to stay she wouldn't be reliant on him, but that her sister would also have space for her, that there was the possibility of a more open relationship with her father, but they were just words. How could he make her see his truth when through fear for herself and love for her sister she'd erected barriers so tall and so thick it would take more than words for Akil to battle through them?

Think, he told himself fiercely. *Think*.

Finally Akil jumped out of the car and half jogged through the streets until he reached his home, letting himself into the apartment where, after quickly feeding Tiger, he rooted around looking for his spare key. Pocketing it, he checked his watch, still not sure if Clem was meant to be heading back to the UK that night, and wended his way through the maze of alleyways behind his apartment until he reached the small jeweller's shop where he and Clem had browsed just a few days before.

The shop specialised in sea glass, and Clem had exclaimed at the beautiful turquoise and greens of the polished jewels. Akil stepped inside and selected a keyring and a matching necklace, quickly paying before jogging back to his car. He slid inside and took the key from his pocket, carefully fastening it onto the keyring, and put the keyring and necklace onto the passenger seat. Right, he had a plan, he just needed the girl.

He pulled out his phone to check it again, his heart speeding up when he saw her name. She was on the beach. That had to be a good sign. He didn't need to ask which beach, quickly starting the car and driving as quickly as he legally could out of the city and across the hilly terrain until he reached the harbour. To his relief he saw her limousine parked up at one end of the car park, Henri leaning against it, the usual inscrutable expression on his face. Akil parked next to it and got out, palming the key and necklace and putting them in his back pocket.

'Is she still here?' he asked, and Henri nodded.

'She went for a walk.'

'How strict are your instructions? Is it a case of getting her to the airfield no matter what, or is there some flexibility?'

'I think they were open to interpretation,' Henri said. 'She'll be safe with you?'

'Always.'

Henri nodded. 'Her bag is in the car.'

It was almost heartbreaking to see how little she had with her, just one small duffel bag that fitted even in Akil's tiny boot. He locked the car and nodded one more time at Henri.

'Thanks for looking after her.'

Akil set off for the beach, standing on the edge and looking out across the sands. It was busy, families gathered for picnics and groups of teens sunbathing and splashing in the waves. He scanned the scene carefully, looking for a single figure walking alone, but couldn't see Clem anywhere. He was going to have to play this one by instinct. He navigated his way through the crowds, until he reached the quieter section a little further away from the harbour. There was still no sign of her.

'Where are you, Clem?' he muttered, looking around, his attention snagged by a piece of material waving in the wind, the same green as the dress Clem had been wearing earlier. He walked over to see the dress neatly folded on a rock, her shoes underneath and, turning, he looked out at the sea. There she was, swimming strong and sure like the naiad he called her, complete in her own natural habitat.

Akil didn't stop to think, unfastening his shirt, kicking off his trainers and discarding his trousers, leaving his clothes in a heap on the sand beside her dress. He walked quickly into the surf and struck out to join her.

The sea was coolly refreshing, filling him with hope and anticipation as he recalled the last time they'd swum together and the time before that—swimming usually ended up with them in bed, salty damp limbs curled around each other. It didn't take him long to reach her; she'd stopped to tread water, her face tilted up to the sky, and he swam up to face her.

'Nice day for a swim,' he said, and she started, submerging for a second then re-surfacing with a gasp. His heart pounded at the sight. She was in her underwear, a pale lemon lace, that clung to her wet curves, her hair sleeked back.

'You scared me,' she said through her splutters.

'I scared you? You're not the one who found a small pile of clothes on the beach with no sight of you to be had,' he pointed out and she smiled up at him.

'I was bored waiting for you and the water looked so refreshing. I feel more like me when I'm in the sea, like a different person, a better person.'

'I'm sure you were a mermaid in a different life.'

'I'm sorry,' she said suddenly, the smile dimmed. 'I am so sorry for what I said earlier today. It's not that I didn't love you, that I don't love you. I do, Akil.'

'I know,' he said—and he did know. Knew with every fibre in him.

'But I was scared. Scared of what my life might be like here if my father decides he doesn't want me here, scared of what my life would be like if you tired of me, if you found me too complicated. Your life is so different from mine, Akil, what you need in a partner is so different from who I am. It's not as if you're unaffected by Court decisions. If my family don't want me around then that will affect you. Affect things that are important to you. I don't want that to happen to you, but, more than that, I don't want to see the look on your face when you realise I'm hampering your career, that I'm in the way. I've seen the look before, you see, on my father's face. I couldn't bear to see it on yours.'

Akil fought to find the right words. 'Clem, you will never see that look on my face, because I will always be proud of you, always want you by my side. I don't know what the future holds for you and your family, although I hope it will be better than what you anticipate, but even if they wanted to banish you completely, never recognise you, I'd still be proud to call you mine. I'll always be proud that you're mine. And you are mine,' he said possessively fiercely, exultant as she nodded.

'I said that all I wanted was someone to love me, and put me first, then here you were offering me just that and I was too terrified to reach out and take it. I'm still scared, Akil,' she admitted. 'I like to project this image of myself as fearless, and in some ways I am, I can go on stage in front of thousands without a single nerve, but when it comes to my heart I'm the biggest coward of all.'

'I meant what I said, Clem. I love you and you will always have a home with me if you want one. I don't want some dull and respectable marriage of convenience to further my career, I want a straight-talking, big-hearted English girl who is happiest in the sea, and thinks nothing of trying to cram twenty activities into one day. I want you and I love you, and I think you and I can do great things here in Asturia; you're already *doing* great things.' He swam closer and touched her cheek, willing his truth into her. 'The work you have started in the hospital is inspiring, Clem. I meant what I said earlier. I'm sure we can find ways to expand it if that's what you want. But if your family make it too difficult for you to be here and that really hurts you, then I'm open to other possibilities. I'm not saying it would be easy, politics isn't really the kind of career that translates well to other countries, but I've had invitations to lecture before and offers of fellowships. I could make it work.'

Clem gazed at Akil wonderingly. 'You would do that for me?'

He smiled into her eyes. 'I hoped you might know by now that I would do anything for you.'

It wasn't just the words, it was the sincerity in his voice and Clem knew that he meant every word, that Akil would walk away from the promise he'd made his father, from the title, from his life here if she asked him to, not because it would be easy or he wanted to, but because her happiness mattered to him. But that kind of strength had to run both ways.

'I don't want to run away. I love it here. I love it here because of you, because of the Asturia that *you* show me, the country that *you* love. The country you dedicate yourself to with your job, with the volunteering you do, with everything you are. How could I not love it? You inspire me with everything you do. I hope that if I stay I can be the kind of asset you need. I'm not really sure how to work a room, but I can learn. It's just another form of acting after all.'

Akil laughed at that, pulling her closer, and she moved in to meet him, her hands on his shoulders, legs entwined as his lips met hers in a brief kiss that sent them both back under the surface. She held onto him as she kicked her way back up, kissing him again as soon as they hit the air.

'My naiad,' he said, smoothing her hair off her face, and she leaned into the caress. 'Could you bear to come back to shore?'

'Maybe this once,' she said, holding his hand as they made their way through the waves back to where they'd abandoned their clothes. It was still so warm that the water began to dry on her skin as soon as they left the sea, and she pulled her dress over her underwear while Akil shrugged his shirt back on, leaving it open. She reached out to run her hand down his chest, enjoying the play of muscles and his intake of breath.

'I've got something for you,' he said, looking uncharacteristically nervous as he picked up his jeans and slid his hand into the pocket. 'I don't want you to feel like you never have a home, Clem. This is yours, for always, to use every day, I hope, but if not whenever you want to.' Clem blinked as she looked at the key, attached to a beautiful turquoise oval of sea glass.

'What's this?'

'It's a key to my apartment,' Akil said, smiling down at her. 'You said the first time you visited that it felt home like. I'm glad you think so because I'd like it to be your home for a while at least. Maybe at some time we could look for a place together, somewhere by the sea, with direct access so you can swim to your heart's content.'

She turned it over, letting the sea glass catch the sun and watching the metal glinting, the symbolism almost more than she could take in. 'You've given me a key?'

'Maybe it's not the most romantic of gifts...'

'It is, it's the most romantic thing I've ever received.' She stepped over the sand and cupped his face in her hands, kissing him fiercely, putting all her love and longing into the embrace. 'It's perfect, Akil, it's absolutely perfect. Thank you, and yes, I would love to have a key to your apartment and yes, I would love to stay there with you and one day move to a house by the sea. I need to go back to Cornwall first. I need to pack up my mother's things and decide what I need and move Gus across. I hope Tiger won't mind a roommate.'

'I know parliament is due back, but I would love to come with you, to see the place you grew up and meet your friends.'

'That would be perfect. I don't believe in ghosts, but the cottage still feels like my mother. I would love her to meet you. I know that sounds silly…'

He slipped an arm around her shoulders. 'It doesn't sound silly at all. I'd be honoured.'

'Oh,' she remembered. 'I have something for you too. I was going to ask Henri to give it to you.' She felt in her pocket and brought out the paper bag. 'I bought it the day we first went on the boat, with matching bracelets for Rosy and me. My mother loved trees the way I love the sea. She always wore nature-inspired things but trees were extra special to her. The very first campaign I remember was her trying to save an old oak from demolition and she got involved with at least two bypass protests—chained herself onto branches and everything. At the time I thought it was totally embarrassing and wished she could just be normal, now I'd give anything to chain myself up next to her. Anyway, I saw these and thought of her.' She handed him the bag and said shyly, 'If you don't like them…'

'I love them.' He held up the delicate cuff-links. 'I'll wear them to the Senate and let myself be inspired by your mother.'

'Be careful, who knows what she'll make you vote for?'

'She raised you, didn't she? I trust her instincts.'

'I think she would like you, Akil Ortiz.' Clem pressed herself close and kissed him, luxuriating in the feel and taste and solidity of him. This wasn't just a fling, this was real, as real as she wanted it to be. She was no fool. She knew relationships needed work and compromise, but she also knew this man was worth it.

'I know it's too early,' he said at last. 'But I want you to know that at some point this year I am going to ask you to marry me. There's a lot to work out, where we'll live, what path we'll take, but as long as we're together we can do it.'

'And I want you to know that I will say yes,' she told him, blinking back happy tears. 'That my home is where you are. I do have one condition…'

'Anything.'

'That once a month we sail away and for at least one night.'

'I'll build it into our marriage vows,' he promised, and she laughed.

'I love you, Akil. Thank you for giving me the space to figure out who I am and what I want, thank you for believing in me. Thank you for loving me.'

'That's the easy part,' he told her and then he kissed her again until she was lost in him. She didn't need a stage or an audience to feel validated any more; she wasn't lost. Thanks to Akil she knew exactly who she was and what she wanted.

'I love you,' she whispered against his mouth and felt him smile.

'And I love you, and I am more than ready to demonstrate how much. Let's go and let your father know that, thank you, but you won't be returning to Cornwall just yet, and then I suggest a few nights at sea, while we get used to this for ever thing.'

'That sounds perfect.' She kissed him again and then, his hand clasping hers, turned towards the harbour. Akil was by her side and had vowed to stay there; she wasn't alone any more. She had a family: a sister and this man. She had a place. She looked up at the late afternoon sky, the sun still beating down, and raised her face to the warmth, sending a moment of love towards her mother, wherever she was, before allowing Akil to tug her towards the harbour. Towards their life together. Their future. She couldn't wait.

* * * * *

Look out for the next story in
The Princess Sister Swap duet,
coming soon!

And if you enjoyed this story check out
these other great reads from
Jessica Gilmore

Winning Back His Runaway Bride
Indonesian Date with the Single Dad
Christmas with His Cinderella

All available now!